T0193361

TEARS

OF A SOUL CATCHER

S. S. SIMPSON

authorHOUSE®

AuthorHouse™
1663 Liberty Drive
Bloomington, IN 47403
www.authorhouse.com
Phone: 1 (800) 839-8640

Published by AuthorHouse   12/19/2019

ISBN: 978-1-7283-4044-9 (sc)
ISBN: 978-1-7283-4043-2 (e)

Print information available on the last page.

Any people depicted in stock imagery provided by Getty Images are models,
and such images are being used for illustrative purposes only.
Certain stock imagery © Getty Images.

This book is printed on acid-free paper.

Because of the dynamic nature of the Internet, any web addresses or links contained in
this book may have changed since publication and may no longer be valid. The views
expressed in this work are solely those of the author and do not necessarily reflect the
views of the publisher, and the publisher hereby disclaims any responsibility for them.

To my beloved Lord who has called me

CONTENTS

THE DEPARTURE

MY FINGERS COULDN'T TEAR THE package open quickly enough. Capturing all of my excitement, Rocky National Park Tour dazzled me. It was the itinerary for the long-awaited trip, a two-week bus tour highlighting the Rocky Mountain National Parks. A single pang of guilt rushed through me. Originally, the trip was planned for two. There was only one name on the reservation. My husband Leon fell and twisted his only leg. Even with the help of his prosthesis, he wasn't able to climb up any stairs or even walk for any amount of time. He wasn't meant to go.

Since we lived in Texas, I hadn't seen anything that wasn't flat for a very long time. To see trees, all together in a forest, would be a sight for my palm-laden eyes. I almost forgot what rocks looked like, let alone a cliff. The attached travel guide gushed of nature and its splendor. I was selfish. Any other person, I was told, would have canceled the trip and waited for a better time when both could go. I couldn't wait. I had to go. Leon couldn't understand why watching the national parks on television wasn't enough. I wanted to see my own country's wonders before the treasures of other countries. Nonchalantly I placed the manila envelope under the other letters. Leon's passion was the mail.

"Is this what I think it is? What you have been waiting for? You aren't really going to go on this trip by yourself are you?" Hoping he wouldn't challenge me, Leon peered at me with questioning eyes. "Sara, I really don't feel good about you going alone. I mean I know you, how you like to wander and explore and often forget about the time. On a trip like this, you have to stay with the group. If you are late, they will just leave you. Then you will have to figure out how you will get back by yourself."

"I know that you don't think that I should go alone, but this is a much needed trip. The nature, the beauty calls out to me. For many reasons, this year at school was more than challenging. What was drained out of me needs to be replenished."

Seventh grade was not the easiest grade to teach, but I chose it because it was my worst year of school. Back then because I didn't know who I was, I didn't like myself or hardly anyone else. Those same uncertainties were in my students. They longed for a sense of stability and some certainty.

"Sara, I just don't want anything to happen to you. It is still difficult for me to believe that your overprotective mother, who calls me non-stop when she can't find you, has agreed to let you go. If I need help, your parents will be there. But no one will there for you."

Leon always made me feel that I violated every written and unwritten rule for a loving marriage. His middle name was worry. It wasn't mine. I knew that I could take care of myself. This thought haunted me for my entire trip.

I handed him the brochure. "Look, this is the itinerary."

By the look on my face, Leon knew that I was already there. If only he could anticipate and get excited about traveling. But he never did. Leon didn't really care if he ever left the house. To him, a trip was just a diversion, another way to spend money, wait on people and practice patience which he didn't have. But to me just mention the word *trip*, and my eyes popped and my mind raced.

Preparing for the trip consumed me. It was such a different kind of trip. Usually when we traveled, we stayed at fancy hotels with fancy pools and fancy restaurants. There was nothing fancy about nature and the wilderness. It wasn't there to entertain you. It was there for you to admire. Lodges and inns tucked in the woods were our sleeping accommodations. Some of the places were so remote that they didn't even have phone access. My phone charger would become my lifeline. Ordinarily I disliked the phone, but this trip would alter that perception forever.

As my departure neared, Leon's apprehension grew like an unwanted weed. Daily he would think of things for me to be concerned about from mosquitoes carrying Bengay Fever to severe leg cramps from too much walking. Nature was foreign to Leon, not to me. Being from New England, I was raised in it, understood it, and knew its obstacles.

The day arrived. On the way to the airport, there were things I know I should have said. I was too excited about what lay ahead of me to remember what I was leaving behind. If only I took more time to assure Leon how much I would miss him, how much I loved him. I would give anything to be back in that car. Before I knew it, good-byes were said, and I got through the winding check-in line without losing anything. On my first try, I discovered that my liquid cleansing products had to be separated in baggies because of the new recent rules regarding flammable fluids on the airplane. In other words, anything that a terrorist might make a makeshift bomb with had to be identified and cleared. But I didn't think my makeup, my mascara, and my lip gloss fell into that category. It did. As I was instructed to go through the line a second time I didn't even know if I would have enough time to make it to my terminal. It was too close. I almost missed my plane. I should have. Circumstance was doing its best to slow me down. I didn't listen closely enough.

Starring out the small window, I focused on what lay below me—tiny rectangular blocks dotted between open gaps of green then everything blurred and swirled away. A window seat calmed me knowing that I could redirect my eyes in something other than a book or a stranger's face. Forced conversation about the weather or the food didn't interest me. I missed Leon already. Flying wasn't my favorite thing to do, but it was necessary for any distant adventure. The very first thing that I did was to make sure that there was an available empty air bag tucked in the seat pocket directly in front of me. I wanted to be prepared. I never ate before a flight or on a flight. I remember once when horrified passengers on both sides of me watched as I heaved only gasps of air. The stares said it all. I felt like a leper out of my colony. Hearing childish voices from the back of the plane, I was thankful they were not next to me. As the plane ascended higher and higher cries vibrated down the aisle. I was not surprised. My Kleenex-stuffed ears blocked it out.

The flight attendants did their best to calm and satisfy. One passenger always wanted more. He sat right next to me. The stewardess certainly got her exercise walking back and forth with his requested drinks. I couldn't help but notice how he inhaled them like water. He felt compelled to tell me why. Ordinarily, I might not have listened but there was nowhere to go.

His pain consumed him. He had been on a grueling business trip and was just fired for no apparent reason. Devastated, he couldn't go home. He couldn't tell his wife. Listening put everything in perspective for me. I felt thankful that I had a job, even though at times it tested every bit of patience in me. It was a smooth descent, but my ears blocked up even with the wads of Kleenex. After the plane halted, the grief-stricken stranger helped me yank down my carry-on luggage from the stuffed cubicle. It was a humbling flight. Thanking the pilot for his expertise, I couldn't help but notice his youthful beaming face. Did they hire twenty-year olds to pilot planes? Had I really aged that much? I quickly dismissed the thought.

LAS VEGAS

THE LIGHTS OF VEGAS HYPNOTIZED, captured, and refused to release you. The airport was so huge; many people were in such a hurry. Until I saw his face, I felt insignificant. There was just something about a brother who cared. I couldn't believe Mark had really taken the time to meet me. It was just so unexpected. He was supposed to meet me later at the hotel. He must have called Leon for my flight arrival.

"Here let me take that."

Mark had always looked out for me and time only cemented our relationship. We seemed to grow closer even though the absence tried to pull us apart. Not wanting to live with the rest of the clan in Texas, Mark opted for Las Vegas. The 110-degree desert was his choice. It didn't matter to him if he lived alone. It mattered to me.

"Mark, how can you stand this heat?" I asked breathlessly.

"Heat, and you are from Texas? At least there is no humidity." Mark grinned from ear to ear.

That was Mark. He never told you what you wanted to hear but what he thought. That is why I respected him. I could count on him. Before I could even think of having a margarita with olives there was one in my hand. Sizzling shrimp and lobster followed, clarifying my thoughts. I didn't know how hungry I was. Piano music wafted around us as the waitress checked on us three or four times. Mark was the attraction. Fascinated, I wondered how Mark had escaped the clutches of marriage. Wanting to know if things had changed, I sounded like a mother.

"Have you spent any significant amount of time with anyone lately?" I quipped, anxious to hear about a new romance. Mark just laughed. He knew how desperately I wanted him to meet someone.

"The work, the job there really isn't any time for anything else."

Mark was his job, a natural-born sales man who could sell anything to anyone at any time. I wished I had his charisma, his easy manner. Strangers flocked to Mark. Like insecticide, I repelled strangers. Maybe this trip would change that. It did in ways that I never would imagine.

After dinner, we sauntered around the casinos and saw heightened, swaying water spouts from across the street. Hurrying, strains of Mozart filled our ears as we watched the water ballet at the prestigious Bellagio Hotel. Excited foreign phrases filled the air as tourists from all over the world oozed and awed. Romance penetrated me. I reached for Leon's hand. It wasn't there. An unaccustomed coldness numbed me. I forced myself to concentrate on the riveting water.

"It's getting late. Sis, you still need to check in, get settled, and meet your tour director. You wouldn't want to miss anything, would you?"

I already did. Tonight the designated tour group was supposed to meet and introduce themselves at a buffet provided by the tour. I couldn't think of anything I would rather miss. Tomorrow would be soon enough to meet forty strangers by myself.

"Mark, are you sure that a two-week bus tour to the national parks with some elderly retirees doesn't interest you?" Knowing what he would say, I still asked him.

"I still haven't figured out why you want to subject yourself to eight hours a day on a bus when you hate buses. Also considering how much you enjoy mingling with strangers, and older ones at that. It is not something that I would even give a second thought." I knew that it didn't make sense, not even to me, but it was the easiest way to see the national parks.

I would see Mark again in two weeks. Checking in was easier than I expected. All I needed was the password, the name of the tour. Hurrying, I still needed to meet the tour director in another part of the hotel. The front desk gave me general directions, but there were six lobbies before I reached the welcoming booth. I was in a maze—all had the same identical elevator in the same spot in every hallway. Just when I gave up, I saw the welcome sign, the table with name tags, and the pensive tour director. Introducing myself, I watched as a short, thin, pale man weakly shook my hand. This couldn't be the tour director. It was. Envisioning a husky outdoor nature type, I hoped I didn't look too startled. Mr. Hudson didn't seem concerned about my excuses for missing the buffet. He was glad that I arrived, and that tomorrow morning my bags would be packed, out in the hallway, and ready to be picked up by six-thirty. Since I was by myself, I even got my own seat and didn't have to share with a complete stranger. Thank you, Mr. Hudson. Relieved, I was in my adventure.

Waking up at five-thirty was easy. It was the same time that I got up on a school day. My bags cooperated. I placed them outside the door, which was a luggage runway. Mr. Hudson cautioned me that if anybody missed the luggage pickup, they carried their own luggage to the bus. Everyone listened.

The coffee bean aroma saturated my senses as I slowly inhaled a cup of strong coffee. Mingling through the lobby were expectant bus tourists who waited for Mr. Hudson. It seemed strange to me that he wasn't on time, and it was only the first day. You could tell who was in the group by the name tags. I didn't put mine on so no one gave me a second look. It was an older group and almost everyone was part of a pair. Pairs rarely mingled with singles. I felt contagious. The megaphone sounded through the lobby Mr. Hudson emerged and quickly made up for any lost time. Before I knew it, I was seated towards the back of the bus. No one balked at the assigned seating arrangement. It was just like school. Clutching his paperwork in one hand and his microphone in the other, Mr. Hudson began lecturing about our first stop, Zion National Park in southwestern Utah. Listening was usually difficult for me, but I found the park's history interesting.

"Eight thousand years ago," Mr. Hudson started, "the Anasazi Indian tribe, also known as the basket weavers inhabited the area. With time, other tribes moved in, The Parowan Fremont, the Parrusits, and other Paiute subtribes." I had never heard of these Indian tribes and decided it would make a great lesson for my curious seventh graders. "In 1858, the Mormons discovered the land. And in 1909, President William Taft designated the canyon a national monument to protect it. The original name was changed to Zion National Park in 1918 by Congress." It had never occurred to me that a park could have its own separate history. "The park is located where the Colorado Plateaus, the Great Basin, and the Mojave Desert meet. Kolob Canyons is the northern part of the park. One of our steepest rivers, the Virgin River flows through the park. There is a six-mile road that leads to The Temple of Sinawava built for the Coyote God of the Paiute Indians." I wondered if I would be able to see the temple. Six miles was a long walk. Mr. Hudson read my mind. "There is a tram along the way for those of you who would rather ride. The canyon narrows at the temple and a foot trail leads to the mouth of the gorge which was twenty feet wide and two thousand feet tall. Keep your eyes peeled for golden eagles, red-tailed hawks, peregrine falcons, and white-throated swifts." This was going to be quite a hike. Most of the older tourists didn't look like hikers, but looks were deceiving. "You will have three hours to explore this park. It tends to be hot out there, so pace yourself and watch your watches."

I couldn't wait until we arrived at the park. The lengthy bus ride nagged at me. I was once again a kid, back at elementary school on the bus. Taking the bus to school made me dizzy and sick but complaining didn't work then and wouldn't work now. At least I didn't have to wait for someone to anxiously plop down next to me. This seat was taken and didn't have to be shared. This was definitely not a single's adventure. There was only one other individual by herself, and she sat directly behind me.

Locking myself in the scenery, I focused and refocused my binoculars on the changes outside my window. Mountain ranges arched themselves behind us, as we made our way into the desert. There was only one single stretched out road and we were on it. Cactus sporting red tequila buds burst on either side of the road. They clung to the reddish earth. The clay colored land was different than Texas, but it was just as flat.

Behind me, I couldn't help but notice raised binoculars. It had to be a single's activity. Within minutes, we introduced ourselves. At least I attempted to be friendly. This was going to be an awfully quiet trip unless I had someone to talk with. As we rambled through the desert, Mr. Hudson briefly mentioned that we would be stopping every three hours. I was more than ready for the break. Our first stop was a grocery store. Sitting on a bus made people starving. Swarming the store, these people looked like they hadn't eaten in days.

I was restless. My legs took over and for fifteen minutes I walked briskly down a country road. Mr. Hudson made it very clear that if you were not back at the bus at the designated time, the bus would leave without you. If left behind, I couldn't imagine how I would ever be able to catch up with the tour. My watch and I became inseparable. Like clocked robots, we quickly boarded the bus. Zion Park waited patiently for us. As the hours pressed on, I was relieved that I was not queasy. My mind opened up considering other thoughts, other questions. Maybe it was the nature, the vast openness; I don't really know, but I was overcome. Then and there I asked the Lord to help me win souls for him. No sooner had I asked I felt an inner peace overtake me. It wasn't long before the Lord answered my prayers.

The wind picked up, and Zion's National Park sign rattled on its post. On the tour bus, individuals just gravitated to one another forming little groups, little cliques. Meg, the single lady, behind me just started jabbering away when we got off the bus. She attended the banquet the previous night and introduced me to a friendly couple she had met from Virginia. I felt an instant connection with Martha. It was the way she phrased things, her cheerful spirit, and her caring actions. It turned out that Martha was a counselor. I could have guessed it. It was something that we all had, an innate charisma that yelled school. Martha's husband, Joel, was a businessman who couldn't get enough of the outdoors. Joel's camera never stopped clicking this way and that. The grueling seven-hour bus ride quickly faded away as the dirt trail stretched out before me. Joel, Martha, and I kept up a steady gait. We were all in good physical shape except for Meg. Hiking was foreign to her. Being from New York, a subway haven, I could understand why. Meg did her best to keep up but lingered behind. The well-trodden trail shadowed the winding Virgin River on our left. It had been years since I watched flowing water. Kicking off our sneakers, we waded in the coolness, skipping on some of the bigger boulders. Childhood rushed in as the rippling water soothed the oppressive 110-degree temperature. Steep, copper-colored cliffs climbed along the riverbed as our eyes and ears awaited bird cries. There were none. It was too hot for birds. Determined to locate a bird's nesting site, Joel disappeared in the thicket heading towards the cliff. The dry heat slowed us down, so we decided to rest under the boughs of an ancient looking tree. The beauty mesmerized me.

"Just look at God's handiwork," I commented. You would have thought I was speaking in a foreign language. Martha acted as though she hadn't heard me. It was her face that betrayed her.

"So you believe in God?" Martha studied me intently as though on a mission. Startled, I caught my breath. Meg cleared her throat more than once.

"Who do you think created all of this?" Martha stared straight through me as though I wasn't there.

"It's evolution, of course. Nature and man have evolved. It is what we believe." Inside, I ached. I hadn't met a nonbeliever in such a long time, and she was a counselor. I wished she wasn't a counselor. It just made it worse. Every counselor I knew thrived because of their faith. I realized why God placed me in this group. Meg purposely kicked some of the trail dirt with her sneaker. She couldn't wait to move.

"It is time to get going. We certainly don't want to miss anything like the temple to the Indian's Coyote God."

Meg didn't want to offend anyone and derailed the conversation with her comment. Plodding down the trail, Martha's words vibrated in my brain. Then I clearly heard Leon's words: "Don't judge." I didn't and focused on the running river. Abruptly, Joel appeared with a contagious grin. Triumphant, he had located a bald eagle's nest perched on a rock ledge on the face of the cliff. His proud pictures captured a mother bald eagle feeding her hungry young. Realizing how tired he was, Joel suggested that we take the tram. One of the tram's designated stops was nearby, so we only had to wait a few minutes. The open-air tram, loaded with passengers, slowed to a stop. There was standing room only. We anchored ourselves preparing for the bumps. My tired legs only wanted to relax. After fifteen minutes, we once again tackled the trail. Joel noticed that Martha was not herself and gently pulled her aside. Their conversation had wings. I overheard every word.

"You seem deflated somehow. Is anything wrong? Is the hiking too much for you?"

"I just feel uncomfortable. I didn't want to get into it on this trip with anyone. But I already have."

"I was only gone for an hour. What could have possibly happened in that time? You were only with two other people that you just met."

"It's Sara. She is one of them."

"One of whom?"

"A Christian. I would just rather not know. It's all over her. That's all I see now when I look at her."

"We have had this conversation before. It doesn't mean you can't be nice to her, does it?"

"I just don't want to have to defend how I feel about things."

"Did she want you to defend your feelings?"

"Well, no it wasn't discussed."

"We have been so looking forward to this tour. Can we please enjoy it? Just forget about it. I am sure Sara won't bring it up again."

Winding upward, the trail took its toll. Our legs felt the steady incline. Still miles ahead, reaching the coyote temple seemed doubtful. Secretly, I was relieved. Pagan animal worship didn't interest me. Others passed us going the opposite way. We were going in the wrong direction, turning around we headed back. There was little conversation as our robotic feet trudged downward. As I reached the end of the trail, a bus never looked so good. With only a few minutes to spare, everyone had made it back on time. Mr. Hudson seemed surprised that no one had reached the temple. Being the youngest group, he thought we would see it. I guess age had little to do with the climb. Exhausted and barely making it to my seat, I sunk down and didn't care how long it took to reach our next destination, Bryce Canyon National Park. At least the next park didn't involve walking, only watching. As Mr. Hudson started his commentary about the park, my ears listened. My aching legs relaxed.

"Bryce Canyon National Park was created by erosion and looks like a giant amphitheater. You will see hoodoos, red, white, and orange sedimentary rocks that have been eroded by wind, water, and ice. These rock colors can be seen in the rock formations, which rise up to two hundred feet tall. Once again the Anasazi Indians were the first to inhabit the area. Anasazi artifacts have been found in the parks that are thousands of years old. The Paiute Indians then settled in the canyon who believed that the Hoodoos were actually legend people that the Coyote trickster had turned into stone. Hoodoos in the Paiute language meant 'red painted faces.'"

The sound of that word, *hoodoos*, echoed in my mind. There was something spiritual about it. The mythology of the Indians certainly made you wonder. Nature affected the Indians and their beliefs. They had to come up with answers to unexplained events. I was thankful that I didn't live back then.

"In 1872, U.S. Army Major John Wesley Powell surveyed the area, and Mormon settlers followed. Scottish immigrants, in particular a Mr. Bryce and his family made it home raising cattle and building roads and canals for irrigation. The canyon was named after a Mr. Bryce. In 1916, the Union Pacific and Santa Fe Railroads wrote about the area in magazines. The railroads expanded to this area to attract tourists. Logging and over grazing destroyed the land so the canyon needed to be protected. In 1923, President Harding made the area a national monument. The federal government purchased state land, and it became a park."

I had never considered how a national park was founded. People were passionate about the land and wanted to maintain it for future generations. So much wilderness, so much beauty. So much to see and it might have all been consumed. Indebted to these settlers, I couldn't wait to tell Leon all about the parks' histories.

Standing on the rim of the canyon and peering through my binoculars, the hoodoos came alive before my very eyes. It was a Martian vista on planet earth. The orange and red rocks were painted with splotches of swirling strokes. The oversized vertical sculpted fingers were carved by an unknown hand. As far as you could see to the left and right were erosion formed figures that were thousands of years old. Silence hung in the air. No sound came from our talkative group. Looking outward, I curiously studied the tossed stone formations. Odd outlines of faint faces were etched in the rocks. Unsettling me, the Indians' beliefs saturated my mind. The more I listened, the more I heard. Something held my eyes, not wanting me to look away.

A frantic yell shattered the spell. Joel slipped off his vantage point wanting the perfect picture of the hoodoos. Reacting quickly, Mr. Hudson selected a few unsuspecting volunteers. Urging them out to the stretched out pinnacle, Mr. Hudson instructed others how to loosen Joel from the clinging debris. Following along, I moved my feet carefully along the rim not looking down. Frantic, Martha watched as nervous hands hoisted Joel to safety. Getting the perfect picture was almost deadly.

As the sun sunk slowly in the chilly orange-marmalade sky, colors changed to a deeper red and musky orange. The hoodoos were transformed. Just as I turned to go, I heard it. It was faint, distant, barely audible. It was a faraway voice. Meg was the only one near me, and she wasn't speaking.

"Meg, did you just hear something?"

"You mean the rubble that Joel kicked half-heartedly down the canyon?

"No, it wasn't that kind of a sound. It was more like a voice."

"Well, there are a bunch of people ahead of us. You know how sound carries especially in a canyon."

"It came from the other side. Maybe it was an echo."

"No, it probably was one of the hoodoos calling out to you." Meg laughed in spite of herself. "You aren't superstitious are you?"

"No, sidewalk cracks and ladders don't bother me."

"Then I guess you don't have anything to worry about." Meg was right. I was probably just worn out from all the hiking and sitting on the bus.

"It has been a long day. I don't know what tired me out more, the bus or the trail. Eight hours on the bus was exhausting."

"I couldn't agree with you more. I thought riding the subway to work every morning was difficult. Now it won't be. My joints feel a little stiff. Maybe it's early arthritis." Tossing her head back, Meg laughed freely. It was spontaneous, contagious. New Yorkers were supposed to be reserved, but Meg was just the opposite, carefree and friendly.

Laughter embraced us as we clamored back to the bus. There was a connection. We were both traveling alone and both from the

East Coast. Talking was easier with someone who wasn't attached to someone else. Within an hour, the bus reached the inn where we would stay for one night.

Once we arrived at the inn, Mr. Hudson distributed the room keys. Surprisingly, our rooms closely followed the seating arrangement on the bus. Choosing your own room wasn't even an option. Unless you had undisclosed physical disabilities, which limited your stair climbing, your room was not changed. I didn't care until I got in my assigned room. There was no television, no telephone, and no reception. We were in the mountains. The room was noisy. Where was the noise coming from? I couldn't figure it out. Conversations from other rooms were seeping through the walls. The walls were not paper thin. They were thick and sturdy as I carefully knocked on them in several areas. It had to be a camouflage heating vent.

Dinner was the only meal included in the package, so I hurried to the restaurant. Going into a restaurant alone was not one of my favorite things to do. When on a trip, you do what others do pretty much without even thinking or caring.

As I returned to my room, I turned the key and cold, mountain air penetrated every inch of me. The walls no longer talked or argued. It was quiet. Six-thirty would arrive very early. Beneath the only window in the room, the wind softly whistled luring me to sleep.

THE CHOIR

SURPRISINGLY, I WOKE UP BEFORE the alarm. Mr. Hudson's pertinent instructions about the luggage bags filtered through my mind. Lugging my own bag down to the bus was not something that I wanted to do. Gazing out the window, early morning sunlight danced briskly off the face of the mountains. Last night's darkness hid the peaks.

Seeing something that wasn't perfectly flat was surreal. I never should have given up the mountains in Connecticut. But in Texas I found Leon. Thinking of him unnerved me. Hopefully, there was cell phone reception in Salt Lake City where we were headed.

Today was Sunday—the only day that the Mormon Tabernacle Choir performed in Salt Lake City. We were supposed to arrive by ten o'clock to hear the live performance. We just made it before the door closed. The Mormon Tabernacle Auditorium held hundreds of people. Feeling privileged just to be here, I scanned through the brochure. The Mormon Tabernacle choir sung for every president since President William Taft. In 2002, the choir performed at the Winter Olympics in Salt Lake City. They were world renown and performed in other countries as well: Central America, Brazil, Israel, Japan, and Western Europe. Often the choir was accompanied with famous orchestras like the New York Philharmonic and the Royal Philharmonic Orchestra of London. Lots of travel involved, I would never make it.

Since it was completely voluntary, each choir member paid for their own travel expenses. The choir also recorded over three hundred recordings. Any money that was earned went to the Mormon Tabernacle

Church. All choir members must be members of the Church of the Latter Day Saints. Definitely a lot of rules in order to sing.

The Mormon religion was founded by Joseph Smith and his successor was Brigham Young. In 1847, the Mormons founded the choir. They needed a place to call their own. In 1867, the Salt Lake Tabernacle met their needs. Their famous organ had over eleven thousand pipes. Hearing the organ billow and the choir's harmony in person would be so different than viewing it on television.

"Did you know that the Mormons are polygamists?" Meg elbowed me as we waited for the choir to start.

"I remember watching a program on television about the Mormons and distinctly recall that there are different factions that don't believe in polygamy."

The tightness eased in Meg's face. Maybe it made a difference. It did to me. I couldn't imagine sharing Leon with anyone else. A tap on Meg's shoulder startled both of us. Apparently Meg's puffy layered hair blocked the lady's view who sat behind her. She politely asked Meg if she could push her hair down a little so that she could view the performance. Meg politely turned around and suggested that the lady move her seat if she couldn't see. Meg didn't seem bothered by the lady's stupid comment. I was horrified. Ignorance showed its ugly face.

Thank goodness there were other faces, expectant faces belonging to numerous individuals in other tour groups, all in rows, all waiting. There was a deafening hush then in unison, one crimson robe followed after one another. The orchestrated rows of choir members stood directly above the orchestra. The lights dimmed, the television cameras rolled, and mouths opened. Mesmerized by the music I almost forgot to record. Recapturing this beautiful harmony was important because I wanted to share it with everyone. Passion rose from the hymns pulling me closer. Another world held me. The surround sound gushed as the organ bellowed deeply. With my binoculars, I could even see the organist pushing the pedals and the transfixed expressions on the faces of the choir members. If I saw or heard nothing else this entire trip, this alone was worth all of the monotonous hours on the bus. Tears seeped into my eyes when I thought of all the deaf impaired who would never have the ability to hear this beautiful music. Thanking God for the ears he gave me, I never again would take them for granted. Our tour group left the auditorium as quickly but not as quietly as we entered.

BLUNT AND ABRUPT

AN OLD WESTERN TOWN ON the Jackson Trail awaited us. Going from angelic music to steer roping cowboys was quite a switch.

Her gold-embossed cross caught my eye. Mrs. Dawner and her husband sat across from me on the bus. Her short grayish cropped hair shifted slightly as the bus came to an abrupt stop. Her greenish eyes focused on my pink sneakers.

"Is this your first bus tour?" she asked, looking as though she wanted to talk. Mrs. Dawner already introduced herself to almost everyone else on the bus. She enjoyed talking. Her husband didn't. Mr. Dawner reminded his wife to sit quietly, but she just couldn't.

"No. My husband and I took a bus tour last summer traveling through the Canadian Rockies. With this trip, there is much more bus time. But I guess it is still easier than renting a car and locating the national parks by yourself."

"Where is he? Two weeks is an awfully long time to be separated from him, isn't it?" Blunt and abrupt was just the way this trip was going to be.

"Leon hurt his good leg days before we were suppose to leave. It curtailed his walking and climbing for any extended amount of time. He didn't want to risk falling. Leon never would have made it. Being in pretty good shape, I can barely make it." A silent sadness filled Mrs. Dawner's eyes.

"Especially when you have a husband, it is hard to be alone. My daughter-in-law is coping with her own loneliness. My son, a navy officer was serving his country overseas in Iraq. Darlene was well aware of his naval commitment before she committed herself to him. Distance was one thing, disease was quite another. Three months ago Edward was abruptly discharged. It wasn't a land mine that devoured him. It was his own body. Edward developed continuous crippling pain and was diagnosed with liver cancer. The doctors, the hospitals..." Clutching her cross, Mrs. Dawner stopped. Her own loneliness burst. "Edward is my only son. I don't want to lose him. I won't lose him. Before my very eyes, my son has faded like a shadow." I saw my own mother and wanted to wrap my arms around Mrs. Dawner. Mr. Dawner just stared straight ahead, his own loneliness pulled him away. "My faith has tried to anchor me. It is all that I really have to hold onto."

"Things happen. Sometimes there are no answers. When Leon was twenty, he was struck by a drunk driver and lost his leg. He suffers with phantom pain. No medication can relieve it. Pain is his life, and he doesn't know why." Pulling my cross out from underneath my sweater, Mrs. Dawner noticed and smiled faintly. I wonder how many other wounded hearts on the bus were waiting to open up.

A seat ahead of me, Meg contentedly drifted off as music filled her ears. Leon filled my ears. I wasn't sure if it was the conversation that I had with Mrs. Dawner or the fact that I hadn't talked with him for two days. Uncontrollable tears slid down my face. It was unexpected. Turning my back to the Dawners, I turned towards the window and tried to think about anything except Leon. There was little privacy on the bus, and the couple behind me couldn't help but notice. Australian accents raced through the air.

"What in the world is that young lady crying about?" A lady's hushed comment reached my ears. A strong male voice continued.

"She certainly is upset about something. I wonder what happened to her."

"I don't care. I didn't pay good money for this trip to have someone quibbling non-stop on the bus. Something has to be done about it."

Their words shocked me. Were these people for real? Did I really hear what I heard? Their coldness numbed me. My tears dried up as I pulled my pink baseball cap down lower over my forehead. This was only the first week of the trip. I thought that I was stronger than this. Hearing more than enough, I remembered my music, centered my iPod, and attached the headset. The symphony embraced me. Once again, Leon was in my arms.

The western town was only one street, but there were two sides. Each storefront was stuffed with western memorabilia. I was back in the 1800s. One shop toted cowboy outfits, boots, guns, and cowboy hats. Imagining Leon in one of them, I almost bought one. It would never survive the rest of the trip.

"Sara, wait up." It was Joel. "Doesn't this just make you want to saddle up a horse and ride off into the sunset?"

"Not exactly. But I can visualize sipping a cool drink at the saloon." I smiled, thankful for Joel's friendliness.

"Well let's go get one. I am a little thirsty myself."

"What happened to Martha?"

"Oh, she disappeared with Meg in one of the shops." Balanced on a stool, I watched as the bartender dressed in a white ruffled shirt, black bow tie, and brown pedal pushers tossed drinks together effortlessly. There were brown-eyed deer heads mounted on the wooden walls, and the jute box clanged out banjo tunes. Joel ordered two mango margaritas. Frothy pinkish lime floated on the top with submerged olives hovering at the bottom of the immense glass. One slushy mouthful followed another, as Joel tapped his fingers to the banjo's melody. Joel centered his stare right between my eyes. I felt like a deer in a blinding headlight.

"Martha mentioned that you were a Christian. How can you believe in God?" I couldn't wait to tell him.

"My life without God would be nothing. When you accept Christ, and have faith something happens. You change, want to read his word, and spend time with him in prayer."

"Well that is just it. How do you know that there is a Christ? I mean that he really is the son of God?"

"You just believe. The Holy Spirit answers all your questions. Once you know Christ, he can never be taken away from you. You depend on him.

"I wish that I knew him. Working as an engineer can be very trying. I no longer enjoy the work load and the long hours. Martha doesn't understand the pressure that I feel. I am afraid to tell her."

"Have you ever opened up the Bible or tried going to church?

"Once, we attended church, but Martha got insulted when someone inadvertently condemned atheists."

"Maybe you could try a different church."

Meanwhile, Martha wondered what happened to her husband. Instinctively she headed for the saloon. Her eyes were seeing things. Was that her husband drooling all over Sara? Stool by stool, Joel's eyes never left Sara's face. Was he even breathing? Watching, Martha just wanted to yank Sara off that stool. How dare she entice her husband. Some Christian, they were all the same. Joel heard Martha's voice and quickly turned around. I suddenly realized this was a powder keg that was just lit.

Martha was suddenly behind us. "I have spent the last hour looking for you. Why didn't you tell me that you were going to the saloon?"

"I didn't really know. It just happened." That did it. Martha's silence muffled me. Unknowingly, I crossed a boundary. Vanishing was all that I wanted to do so I did.

"There were some other shops that I wanted to explore, so I will see you both later."

"Sara, don't forget that we are only here for another hour," piped Joel, wishing he could leave as well." Martha would never believe that they were just talking about God. Nothing else. Joel didn't even bother to tell her.

Everywhere I turned there was a warning sign. Getting along with strangers was even more difficult than getting along with teachers. Thirsty or not, I knew better than to go off with someone's husband. Martha needed an explanation. It would have to wait. After inhaling that margarita, I also knew that it was time to eat and looked for a restaurant's swinging sign.

Toting two stuffed packages, Meg's arms looked like they ached more than her feet. She was just a half block a head of me.

"Are you hungry?" Meg was a breath of fresh air. As we found that sign, wafts of smoked meat filled my senses. It was a popular restaurant. Almost every seat was taken. Before I knew it, plates of steaming barbecue were placed in front of us. Then through the partition, an irate woman's voice couldn't be silenced.

"I do not want to hear her crying anymore. You are the tour director. Do something about it."

Almost choking on my meat, I took at huge gulp of tea. Meg didn't hear it. My face probably matched the red in the tablecloth. It stopped as suddenly as it started. Of all the people to sit next to us, it had to be the bothered Australian couple from the bus. As the waitress brought them their check, Mr. Hudson stood up, saw me, and his face turned redder than the tablecloth.

I didn't know who was more embarrassed. Mr. Hudson was well aware that my husband was an educator, a professor who wouldn't put up with any of this nonsense. He better stop it before it got off the bus. A tour director needed to know what happened on his bus. Was he that removed? My thoughts were rudely interrupted.

"Sara, Martha is so friendly, so energetic, so easy to get along with," commented Meg. Again I gulped a big gulp of tea. Confiding in Meg, I told her what just happened at the saloon.

"It is your blonde hair. It unglues them. If I had a husband, I wouldn't want him alone with you either," Meg smirked. "Forget about it. Maybe it was just this western air."

Smoothing out the saloon ripples, Meg couldn't wait to show me what was in her bags. I wanted to tell her about the annoyed Australians. But one western story was enough.

Meg could take care of herself and anyone else. She was short, stout with broad shoulders, and didn't care what her hair looked like. It was refreshing to meet someone who didn't have to check her face in a mirror every hour. Meg knew who she was and who she wasn't. I hoped some of her tough self-assurance would rub off on me.

As Meg and I ambled up and down crude dirt paths in town, I noticed how the tour couples paired up as though they had known each other all of their lives. Even the irritated Australians, the Taylors, attached themselves to an unsuspecting pair—a short-haired very young tanned mother in a very short white skirt and her conservatively dressed daughter. Recognizing the pair from the very back of the bus, Mr. Taylor introduced himself much to Mrs. Taylor's surprise. With arms draped around one another, Mr. and Mrs. Taylor seemed inseparable. The eighty-year-old couple became immersed with the young girls. At first, Mrs. Taylor couldn't take her eyes off that white skirt. Then realized Wilehmina probably wouldn't like anything more reasonable. Right before my very eyes, I witnessed an alliance. Infected with Mrs. Taylor's anger, the young girls tossed their heads, laughed, and stared straight at me. Mrs. Taylor was victorious before I even had a chance to defend myself. Being a school teacher, I could sense a bully a mile away. I knew what damage a bully could do in a very short amount of time. Mrs. Taylor needed to be stopped one way or the other. But our time in the town was nearly up. Kicking off the dust, we headed for the bus.

"Sara can I speak with you for a moment?" Mr. Hudson casually asked as Meg joined the others. "Are you feeling alright? I mean you aren't sick or anything, are you?" Mr. Hudson paused patiently waiting for my answer. I was on a slimy slide under a microscope. I flicked the microscope off.

"This is about Mrs. Taylor, right?"

"Yes and no. You know traveling alone isn't the easiest thing to do. I know. I do it all the time. It's hard being away from your family. Missing someone can be overwhelming." I decided to make it easier for Mr. Hudson.

"You are probably right. Last night, I couldn't talk to Leon because of the reception problem with the mountains. On the bus, there isn't much privacy as you know. Once we get to the lodge, I can't wait to talk to Leon and tell him all about Mrs. Taylor and her antics."

"Sara, look. I am sorry that you are upset. However, Mrs. Taylor wants a quiet bus ride. I don't want to have to talk to her again for any reason unless it is an emergency. This is not an emergency." I noticed how Mr. Hudson softened after I mentioned my husband. Then I saw the flash of plastic tucked in his ear partly obscured by his thinning hair. Mr. Hudson could barely hear. He was vulnerable. This was his job. I wasn't going to make it any more difficult than it already was.

"Mr. Hudson, Mrs. Taylor will have her quiet ride."

"Thanks, Sara. Enjoy the rest of the day." As Mr. Hudson readjusted his hearing aid, his shoulders relaxed. When we got to the bus, Mr. Hudson abruptly announced that there were no assigned seats for the remainder of the day. No one moved except the Taylors. The Australian weight against the back of my seat vanished. In front of me, Meg who looked tired but wasn't as she talked non-stop on the phone with a very close friend in Finland. Meg, like me, wasn't really alone, just traveling alone. Since Meg's conversation was mostly in broken Finnish, she wasn't concerned if anyone listened. No one did.

THE RIVER

LEON'S WORDS HOVERED NEAR MY heart.

"Sara, I was just about to get on a plane and come get you. I have called everyone, your parents, no one has heard from you. Why haven't you called? Why don't you just get off that bus and come on home? Feeding our twelve cats by myself is harder than I thought. I don't remember who came up with this trip idea, but you are not going off by yourself again."

Rarely did I agree with Leon. This time I did. When I told him about Mrs. Hudson, his rage reached through the phone. No one bothered his wife. Leon demanded to talk with Mr. Hudson right then and there. Assuring Leon that I could handle the situation, I was thankful that Mr. Hudson was three floors away.

Last night floated quickly by. I couldn't wait to raft down this Snake River, which lay right in front of me. My feet were anchored on a floating rubber raft that was shared by six other rafters bundled up in orange life preservers. Our knowledgeable guide was young, eager, and ready to steer us through the river. With a long wooden oar, Tim pointed out the Grand Teton Mountain range that was on our right shoulder as we floated by. The beauty of the park ensnared us.

"The Grand Teton Mountain is the second highest peak in Wyoming at 137,775 feet high." The majestic, partly snow covered mountain towered effortlessly above the other mountains. "No one knows for sure how the mountain was named. It was either named by French Canadians or Iroquois members of a climbing expedition. Some think it was named after the Native Americans, the Teton Sioux Tribe."

It just added to the mystery of the grandeur I thought. "The mountain is a favorite for climbers. In the winter, skiers and snow boarders also enjoy the mountain's challenge."

Pine trees dotted the mountain's lower basin. The raft's speed picked up as we approached the rapids.

"Do not get up or shift your weight until we get through the rapids."

I couldn't imagine that anyone would even think of doing that. When we boarded at the docking station, the rafts were filled randomly according to who was ready to go. As I looked around, I didn't recognize hardly anyone. Couples breathed in the nature, smiled, and enjoyed themselves. Complaining wasn't allowed. The river wooed us taking us into the surrounding woods. Silvery birches yielded obscured bird nests and red berry saddled bushes. A mother deer and her fawn scratched against the grey-white bark pulling strips of bark off with their teeth.

"Keep your eyes peeled for a moose. It is the perfect weather for them," exclaimed Tim who wouldn't trade his summer rafting job for anything in the world.

"Tell me, Tim, how in the world did you get involved in river rafting," questioned Mr. Thomas, a bespeckled elderly man keenly aware of how difficult it was to maneuver this raft down the river.

"I love this river. All the arduous training that I had to do was worth it. My arms and legs now know just what to expect. The beauty drowns you. I want people to know what is on, near, and surrounding this pristine river. Natural beauty is easily taken for granted and in an instant can be destroyed. Nature demands respect. Here, you feel it. I was raised here, and I want to give back to the land. In the summer, trailing up these mountains, and in the winter, skiing on them changed me. The river continually reveals things. Each time I raft down the river I notice something that I missed. Three of my buddies started an eco-friendly business, making paper from waste material rather than trees. Eventually I want to join their company after I complete my last year at the university."

Tim's concern and determination were refreshing. Tim's philosophy echoed in my own ears. At school, paper was readily wasted. When you were out of it, you just went to the supply room and got another package. It was accessible. It wasn't endless. I realized how much the environment provided, every tree, every river, every mountain mattered. It was more than beauty. I would take better care of it. Tim was a mouthpiece for his passion. What better way to promote his cause as he piloted a simple raft down the winding Snake River in the remote wilderness.

The Snake River prompted conversation between us. Perched next to me on the floor of the raft was a young lady whose binoculars accidentally brushed against my leg. I didn't care. She was bothered and apologized. Recalling her face, I remembered meeting Percy back at the hotel at the registration table. At the very last minute, Percy just decided to take a much-needed vacation by herself since none of her friends could go. There was still room on the bus, so Mr. Hudson welcomed her.

Percy was uncomfortable on the raft's floor but the thought of changing her position was even more uncomfortable. Being underweight, it probably wouldn't have mattered at all.

"It's Sara, right?" I softly heard Percy ask as she turned towards me. "We are two of the three single women on this tour." She was right. I forgot that Percy was a member of the elite group. Had she met Meg, I wondered. Percy's friendliness was contagious. The three other couples included us in with their conversation.

"Percy, how in the world do you keep yourself in such great shape?" asked Mr. Thomas as his extended stomach growled beneath his life preserver.

"In my profession, it is common, expected, demanded. I am an assistant fashion designer surrounded by hungry, svelte figures. My models will not look better than I do." Percy seemed pleased that Mr. Taylor had noticed. Mrs. Taylor didn't seem as pleased.

Mrs. Simon, who sat on the opposite side of the raft, almost toppled over as Tim's oar sank deeply in the water. If her legs went in opposite directions, she would have fallen overboard if Tim had not intervened. In some strange way, that relaxed us as we all told stories about silly things that almost happened. Cool, refreshing river water sprayed everyone almost equally. There was something primitive about a raft. I could almost imagine Lewis and Clark as they sauntered through the wilderness.

"There she is over there." The voice hurdled out at me from deep inside the woods. I just assumed there were hikers trying to locate one another. Then I heard it again rising above the woods as if mounted in the air. "In the raft, she is in the raft." Then I almost toppled and fell overboard. It was an announcement rather than a statement. Tim must have heard it. Maybe someone was in trouble and needed one of us. It had to be another guide, or maybe it was even Mr. Hudson. I waited. Nothing happened. Tim kept oaring. No one else was concerned. Uncertainty crept close to me. No one else had heard it. Why not? Could it have been my imagination? Could it have been the shifting motion of the raft when it turned to the right and the left? It didn't make any sense. I wasn't tired. I slept well last night and even had breakfast. But I heard something. Something clearly. Was everyone pretending that they didn't hear it? Why? The eerie voice echoed in my ears. I just wanted to talk about it. I didn't.

Within an hour's time, Tim artfully reached our final destination on the river, the landing dock. Tim carefully eased the raft to one side of the dock. One by one we removed our orange life preservers and clamored over the raft's side onto the sturdy dock. With both of my feet firmly on the ground, it felt odd not having something move beneath me. When Percy reached into her pocket, I reached into mine. Everyone else followed suit. It wasn't expected, but it was appreciated when dollar bills found their way into Tim's pocket. Loving the river and making a living from the river were two separate things. All of us wanted to make sure that Tim was successful at both. Percy lingered behind talking with Tim. I lingered behind needing an answer.

"Did either of you happen to hear anything out of the ordinary about twenty minutes ago as we rounded the last bend?"

"Beauty." Tim smiled as Percy shook her head.

"What kind of a sound?" asked Percy, surprised that I had stayed behind.

"It sounded like a voice looking for someone." Tim's eyes queried me without a word. "Could it have been hunters deep in the undergrowth?" I continued.

"It could have been, but this area is a national park and hunting is prohibited. Illegal hunting isn't worth the consequences of a hefty fine and or jail time. Most people wouldn't risk it."

I forgot that we were in a national park. When Tim departed, Percy questioned me further about the voice, assuring me that it could have been anything or everything. My doubts diminished as Percy's infatuation with Tim grew. She wanted to raft down the river one more time. There wasn't time. There was no one special in Percy's life. I was thankful that there was someone special in mine.

After all the rafters were safely accounted for, Mr. Hudson seemed very relieved. He was ultimately responsible if anything happened to anyone. Most of the rafters were tired but relaxed and content. Even Mrs. Taylor had a smile on her face. Deep in conversation, Percy and I became friends. We both wanted to sit up front and hoped the seating arrangement could be altered. On the bus, the two front seats were the most coveted spots with their panoramic views. I decided to intervene.

"Mr. Hudson is there any way that Percy and I could sit up front tomorrow since we will be headed for Yellow Stone National Park? I don't want to miss anything and trying to crane my neck form left to right doesn't give me enough time to adjust my camera." My deep dark blue eyes waited patiently for an answer. How could he say no?

"Sara, that will be fine. Let's go ahead and plan on it."

There was something else on my mind. "I noticed a box of books on the bus crunched next to Howard's seat. He was leafing through one when we got off the bus. The cover caught my eye. Could I look at one? I have just finished writing a book myself and am waiting to hear back from the publishers regarding the layout of the cover."

"You are a writer?" I should have known. Writers never want to miss anything. I am also a writer. It is a travel guide about Alaska, its history and spots of interest I used to live there. It took me four years to compile the information and got it published." Mr. Hudson looked at me differently. We were both writers. We understood one another. I knew that I wouldn't have any more trouble with Mrs. Taylor or with anyone else for that matter. Warmth rushed in. I was no longer alone on this bus. I wanted to know all about Mr. Hudson's book, how he wrote it, how he gathered his information, his process.

Unbelievably, I got my chance that very evening. Once we were settled in the lodge, a pre-arranged dinner was scheduled for seven o'clock. When I walked into the dining area, there was Mr. Hudson at an empty table with an empty seat. I promptly filled it. I was on a mission. Everyone looked surprised except for Mr. Hudson who expected it. Mr. Hudson usually tried to converse with several guests at meal times. Tonight his ears and eyes were fastened on me. He wanted to know all about my book and why I wrote it. As I passed the buffet table a second time, I couldn't help but see Martha's eyes locked onto me as if to say there she is with someone else's husband again. After we dissected our books as only authors could, a tired Mr. Hudson excused himself as I thoroughly enjoyed another piece of German chocolate cake. A bizarre conversation reached my ears.

"Look at her work this room. As if it is all about her."

"She really looks nice tonight. Her hair shines in the firelight. Her manners are impeccable. Did you see how she conducted herself? A perfect lady. You would never know it by the way she acted on the bus. Shorts and sneakers every day as if she wore a uniform. Martha better make sure that she keeps Joel away from Sara or by the end of the trip she will no longer have a husband."

That did it. I heard enough. I turned around but there wasn't anyone that close to me. The Taylors were sitting across the room with Wilhemina who was enjoying herself. Most everyone else had already left the room. If someone had something to say about me they needed to say it to my face.

When Meg propped herself down at my table, my resentment faded. Listening to Percy at dinner, curious Meg wanted to know more about the bits and pieces about our wonderful rafting guide, Tim. I knew nothing about the bits and pieces. I was married too long. Disappointed, Meg then told me that Martha and Joel exchanged abrupt words at dinner and even before dinner. Meg's room happened to be close to theirs. Evidently, they weren't getting along very well.

Gossip didn't interest me. I wanted to hear a loving voice full of good news and caring.

"You did what?" was all that I heard as Leon screeched into the telephone. "You need to start thinking, Sara, if you want to make it back home safely from your trip. Jealous women are capable of doing anything."

"I was thirsty and just wanted something cool to drink."

"Was it worth it? Sara, don't you understand? Martha doesn't want to have anything to do with you. You have to promise me that you will leave that couple alone. Do I make myself clear?" And I thought talking to Leon would warm me up. I was a frozen iceberg.

"Sara, you are just so naive when it comes to real life. Since I am not there, I can't protect you. You know the saying about a woman's wrath. Please think about what I have said. Don't talk to any other men on that tour even if they are standing next to their wives." I would find out the next day that Leon's warning came much too late.

SMELLY SULFUR

AS SOON AS I STEPPED on the bus I noticed it. It was quiet, too quiet as if a told secret were known by all. I didn't care. The front seats overpowered the chilly silence. Percy and I were ready, eager, with cameras in one hand and binoculars in the other. When Meg passed by my seat, her spontaneous grin was nowhere to be seen. Little did I know what that meant.

Earlier this morning, Martha filled Meg's ears with allusions. Something about Sara being after her husband. Was she kidding?

Sara always talked about her husband, her professor and just how much she missed him. The only thing linking Sara and Joel was an unwanted pest. Joel annoyed Sara. Sara needed to know about the lies.

As Mr. Hudson clamored into his seat, he couldn't escape the eager grins on our two faces. Seated in the front, we were both in our element. Other couples on the bus seemed oddly quiet. Usually there was excitement in the morning as tourists compared notes on the given destination. Mr. Hudson turned up his hearing aide, wanting to stir up some positive energy. Alluring facts about Yellowstone National Park peaked our interest. Our eyes didn't leave his face. The rest followed suit.

"On March 1, 1872, Ulysses S. Grant signed into law the establishment of Yellowstone National Park. Did you know that the park is located in three different states? Well it is. Most of the park is in Wyoming, but some stretches into Montana and Idaho as well. It was the first national park created by congress. Old Faithful is probably one of the most famous geysers in the world. Underneath it lays the Yellowstone Caldera, the largest super volcano in the United States."

If old Faithful erupted, every hour there was a heat source underneath the surface. But a volcano? Suddenly I felt a great deal of respect for the park and everything in it. No wonder the mud bubbled and so many miniature geysers gushed everywhere you looked. Viewing Yellowstone on television was one thing, but seeing it in person was unforgettable.

"The park has quite a unique history. For the last eleven thousand years, native Indians lived in the region. Yellowstone River was named after French trappers who originally named the river 'Roche Jaune,' which meant Rock Yellow River. Arrowheads of Yellowstone obsidian were found. In 1805, the Lewis Clark Expedition stumbled on the Crow and the Shoshone Indians. One of the explorers, John Colter described the land steaming with fire and brimstone with boiling springs, yellow rock, petrified trees and spouting water. It was then nicknamed 'Colter's Hell.' The Civil War ended exploration. In 1871, Ferdinand Hayden who was sponsored by the government made his own survey. It had photographs and paintings of the area. Congress withdrew the land from public auction. Hayden wanted others to be able to enjoy the beauty and protect the animal and plant life. The land became a national park. Poaching and vandalism were common place. Loggers wanted to log, miners wanted to mine, and hunters wanted to hunt, so the park's size was reduced. In 1886, the U.S. Army built Camp Sheridan at Mammoth Hot Springs."

"Sara, I thought I had trouble with management," commented Percy, enthralled with the historical facts. It is nice to know that the army got involved with saving something rather than destroying something. Given the vastness of the territory, I guess that it was a good thing that the army got involved." Sounding just like a teacher, Percy missed her calling, I thought. Mr. Hudson continued clearing his throat.

"In the 1880s, a train station was built by the Northern Pacific Railroad in Livingston, Montana. Camp Sheridan eventually became Fort Yellowstone. The National Park Service was created in 1916. In 1918, the army decided to give the National Park Service control over the area. During this time, horse drawn buggies were competing with cars. By 1941, park roads, camp grounds, and early visitor centers were established. World War II decreased the stays. Unfortunately in 1959, the most powerful earthquake ever recorded struck."

Listening to Mr. Hudson, I realized that there was much more involved to being a tour director than just registering people and securing accommodations. You had to know facts, everything about anything. The facts continued.

"On August 20, 1988, 'Black Saturday' blackened 150,000 acres of the park with raging flames and gusty winds. Over 1,000 archeological sites, like Obsidian Cliff were discovered in the park."

Taking care of a national park seemed monumental. At school, I was glad I only had to take care of thirty students per class per day. Nearing the end of his presentation, Mr. Hudson was pleased knowing that each time he gave his talk it improved.

"The park is located on Yellowstone Plateau at an elevation of 8,000 feet above sea level. Mount Washburn is the highest point at 10, 243 feet." I could feel the bus climbing as Mr. Hudson spoke. "There is one of the largest petrified forests in the park. Trees were changed to mineral deposits by ash and soil. When you are hiking, keep your eyes peeled for numerous waterfalls and rivers, which are over 640,000 years old." Eager eyes dimmed.

"Sara, I think that I could write a brochure about Yellowstone Park," whispered Percy.

"I know, but now when we walk through the park we know who and what went before us."

From the very back of the bus, applause broke out. It was Wilhemina and her daughter Sky and the Taylors. Mr. Hudson beamed as the rest of the passengers joined in. Waking up, they were once again his tour group.

Martha's vengeance radiated throughout the bus. Her face looked like it would burst. Joel was silent and seemed to distance himself from his jealous wife. He listened intently to the history of the park and turned his wife's voice off.

Joel abruptly blurted out, "I am moving up front."

He seized the opportunity. Recognizing Mr. James from breakfast, Joel slipped in beside him. Eagerly setting up his camera's lenses, Joel became absorbed in the cliff's faces. Surprised with the sudden company,

Mr. James moved over becoming equally enthralled with the cliff's presence.

Meg was stunned and couldn't believe that Joel had moved up front almost in Sara's lap.

A steep incline commandeered the bus. The bus lurched forward as if it had a mind of its own. Off to the right, there was a deep ravine. Everyone wanted to see the rushing river tearing through it. The towering steepness of the cliffs rose steadily as the bus rounded a tight hairpin turn. God stole my heart. I never saw anything as beautiful as this in my life. Martha's jealousy was forgotten.

"Sara, did you get that shot, the lone moose grazing at the base of that cliff?" Joel queried, just wanting Sara to know that he was not part of Martha's anger. Feeling guilty, Joel knew that he should have supported Sara at the saloon, but he didn't. Joel knew his wife's wrath.

I couldn't believe my ears. I didn't believe my ears. It was Joel. Why? Because of him...

"I saw it," I replied. Joel and his camera were off limits. My respect for Joel was swept away with his silence. A mother deer and her fawn sauntered across the road. The bus halted. The brown-eyed couple owned the road. Even with twenty years of experience, Howard had some difficulty skillfully pulling the bus over on the shoulder of the road. It was a private showing. The mother deer nudged her fawn one way, but the fawn insisted going the other way. Just like any kid, I mused. Howard initiated a fifteen-minute camera moment. It was good to stretch my legs. Meg avoided me completely while Martha avoided Joel. Our once happily banded group disbanded. After the brown-eyed couple safely crossed the road, Meg stood almost next to me.

"Sara, whatever you do stay away from Martha. She is not herself right now." Meg looked like she wanted to say more, but she didn't. It was time to re-board. We were almost at Yellowstone. Dropping the window down, I could almost smell the sulfur. Meg's behavior was unexpected. Her comment was even more unexpected. I was certain that Meg was contaminated with Martha's madness. She wasn't.

At school, I witnessed anger almost every day. With the girls, pulling hair, scratching, kicking, punching was not uncommon. Jealously was common. I often had to separate the sickening brutality. Girls fought dirty as boys. Unintentionally, I learned how to protect myself. In my wildest imagination, I just couldn't envision Martha jumping me. I wasn't going to give her an opportunity. It was inconceivable for a grown woman to entertain twelve-year-old thoughts.

Yellowstone's welcoming sign greeted us in forest fashion with bold green-and-gold lettering. The pine trees' scent was natural perfume invigorating my senses. Another odor choked my senses reminding me of a chemistry lab experiment gone terribly wrong. Looking for rotten eggs, I found none. Instead, as far as the eye could see there were miniature geysers spewing out boiling, puffy mists of smelly sulfur.

"Don't forget that Old Faithful erupts on the hour, every hour," Mr. Hudson reminded us as we eagerly departed, going in separate directions.

So much to see, and we only had an afternoon. Searching for authentic Indian-made turquoise jewelry, I eagerly headed for the log cabin gift shop, which bellowed warm winding smoke from rustic stone fireplaces. Percy hurried along beside me. Orange, tangerine scents wafted around every corner. Wanting to bring back pieces of my trip from every park, I carefully studied what was around me. Things were wrapped in fur, or carved in wood or stone, assembled by Indians from various reservations. Turquoise was in belts, vests, hats, wallets, and jewelry in anything that could be worn. Indians in their native dress with white-eagle-feathered head dresses demonstrated their artistic talents.

Native American music was spilling out of hidden speakers. The wooden flutes echoed aching wooden tones. I heard the war cries. I felt the tribal loyalty, the brief joy, the impending sadness, the mounting despair, and the inflamed anger. Defeated sounds wrapped around me. I too was bareback on that horse. The horse's heaving and tightened muscles centered me on its back. Holding on to its streaked mane, I heard the wind whip past my face. Smoke filled my nostrils. Our village was in flames. The white man lay just ahead of us. My desperate heart burst.

The Indians suffered. Hatred still hid in their eyes. Down the hallway, an Indian squaw weaved contentedly. Curiously, I walked towards her. Aged brown fingers commanded the course wool. Her brown eyes were not comfortable with scrutiny. A dreamcatcher, an eagle's feather attached to two pieces of colorful yarn wrapped around wooden sticks, hung near her. Pulling the dream catcher towards her, she spoke of its spiritual powers, how it captured bad dreams when she was a little girl. She motioned me to come closer.

"Hold it in your hands. You will need this," she quietly said, closing her eyes, chanting. For a few minutes, she didn't open her eyes. Her words, her actions puzzled me. Giving her more than enough money for the dreamcatcher, I watched as she slipped it into a plain paper bag. As I turned to leave, she wouldn't look at me. Indians were devout in many of their beliefs. Maybe the dreamcatcher would help Leon's restless periods of sleep. I was a sound sleeper. I didn't need a dreamcatcher. I was wrong.

Hurrying, I moved back towards the music. The turquoise jewelry glistened in the showcase. I didn't know which item to examine first. A young Indian girl did her best to show me several bracelets. After trying on many, I saw it. It was turned on its side, and I wasn't sure what it was. A silver-inlaid turquoise watch was waiting for my wrist. A watch might as well be a showpiece as well as a timepiece. This one would cause heads to turn. Once I fastened the clasp, the turquoise caught the light, heightening the deep, natural, greenish-blue hues. I looked into the depths of a cold ocean stirred by foaming waves. The watch belonged on my wrist. Usually I found something that I wanted first. It wasn't intentional. It was time to think of others.

"Sara, you bought it. I just wanted to look at it one more time. Are you sure it isn't too much turquoise for you?" asked Percy playfully.

"It is just about perfect," I answered knowing that the watch already improved my mood. Martha wouldn't dare attack me with a new watch. Confidence surged inside me. Percy eagerly showed me some of her findings. A small wooden box intrigued me. It was made of hand-carved mahogany with nature etches on the lid. Secretively, Leon loved little boxes. I had to get him one. I quickly purchased two turquoise inlaid key chains that had the exact initials of my brother and father etched on them. My mother was more difficult to surprise. She usually made me return anything that I got for her. Wyoming was a bit far even for my mother. How could my mother not love this beautiful turquoise necklace with matching earrings? After purchasing thoughtful gifts, my selfishness relaxed.

Getting gift cabin fever, Percy and I wanted to explore the natural beauty of the park with all of the bubbling geysers. Full of energy and expectation, we eagerly headed towards one of the well-traveled paths trailing up the mountain. Lagging behind, Percy seemed winded by the hiking. My sneaker-laced feet raced ahead. The winding mountain trail gradually rose in steepness.

"Sara, wait up," Percy yelled, unable to make her high-heeled accustomed feet grab onto the loose shifting rocks on the trail. I didn't want to wait. Arching trees, enormous mica-filled rocks, lingering waterfalls, and shrill-voiced coyotes awaited me. "You can't slow down, can you?" Percy smiled, secretly glad that she had a reason to turn back.

Out of breath and fairly exhausted, she stopped. "I will catch up with you later. Enjoy the mountain." Percy didn't mix her words. Relieved, I was secretly glad that she turned back.

There was something about being alone on a mountain. Pushing, you walked as fast as you could until your legs ached, inhaling the stillness. Mountains were not strangers to me. When I was ten years old, my father and I skied on them.

Up ahead, there were lookout points along the cliff's ledges. Peering down, the height grabbed me. A little light-headed, I rested on a poised wooden bench ready for strangers. Erected five feet away from the cliff's edge was a boundary line. You were not supposed to cross it. I didn't. Time faded as I climbed higher and higher. The sun's blinding rays were no longer in my eyes. The trail was deceiving. The top was nowhere in sight. Alarmed, I realized how much time had passed.

Eager to see Old Faithful and the other spewing miniature geysers, I headed back down expecting the sudden twists and turns. Departing from the woods, I spied trails of spiraling gases that clung in the air. My nose led me to a bubbling cesspool of colors. The copper-filled earth was stained with red, green, and yellow hues as spewing sulfur boiled over it. Raw, eerie, and beautiful, a cratered landscape from a science-fiction thriller surrounded me. The sleeping volcano under my feet added suspense. A smoking ring of geysers partially hid a small lake.

There wasn't a single bird anywhere. I wasn't surprised. The rancid odor would deter anything except of course tourists.

Off towards the horizon, a tremendous spew of gases erupted. Old Faithful awoke. I needed to get there. Confused, I was somehow turned around. Certain areas of the park were roped off, and you couldn't cross them. Each hiker who passed me suggested that I take a different route. Frustrated, I climbed over the ropes and tiptoed across slippery bubbling soil hoping that I wouldn't sink. After several thwarted attempts, the quick sand relented, and I finally crossed over. My sneakers would never be the same. Smelling burned rubber, I looked in horror as parts of the rubber on the bottom of my sneakers still smoked. The area had been cordoned off for a reason. The sign "Hike at your own risk" referred to conditions above the ground as well as conditions below the ground.

Finally, Old Faithful gushed majestically in front of me. The surrounding arena was jam packed. The rustic circular benches were filled with expectation. I thought that I saw Percy but didn't. Digital cameras clicked continuously. Luckily my camera's batteries still worked. Capturing the spontaneity consumed me. Leon would see the restless awe. Within five minutes the roar of spewing water stopped. As if on cue, the bubbling water slipped back into the crater not to be seen again for another hour. Talk about being on a schedule.

Getting away from the tour group for a few hours completely refreshed me. With only twenty minutes left, I realized I saw more of Yellowstone than I thought. Returning to the bus meant returning to cramped emotions. Thirsty, anything cold would do. I headed for the food tent. While waiting in line, a sudden push from behind caused me to lose my footing. An icy cold liquid ran casually down my back. My adrenalin rushed for nothing.

"I didn't see you," a young voice stammered. Two serious blue eyes peeked at me from under the rim of a brand new bear engraved Yellowstone baseball cap. Tussled brown curls covered his red, embarrassed ears. A young boy had slipped away from his mother's grip. How could I be upset? Assuring the young boy that no harm had been done, I bought a cherry soda myself consuming it the right way. With an unexpected cherry stain on the back of my shirt, I hurried. I wasn't going to leave without it.

Leon needed to hear the Indian music. The spiritual lyrics would challenge him as he recreated them on his guitar. Oddly, Leon and I both had Indian uncles. My favorite uncle was part Cherokee. Uncle Sik hardly laughed. He hardly smiled. I could never tell what he was thinking. But he thought a great deal. He was a judge. Since hearing the tribal sounds, thoughts of Uncle Sik lingered. I just couldn't get him out of my mind. Struggle was not foreign to him. He was a prisoner of war in Korea for five years. Nothing stopped him, not even losing most of his hearing. His wife became his ears when she accompanied him to law school. Uncle Sik couldn't be defeated and became a federal magistrate. His determination refocused me.

This was just a two-week trip. Half of it was gone. Regardless of what did or didn't happen, I was going to enjoy the remaining week. After all, it was supposed to be fun. Time away from Leon would make me stronger. But right now, I would give anything to talk to him.

The overnight lodges looked the same, rustic, hidden, obscured by mountains, and far away from civilization. Tired from so much hiking I usually didn't care. Tonight I did.

"Her blond ponytail sticking out from under her cap is just asking to be trimmed." Shuddering, I moved closer to the heating duct. "It would be so easy to do. No one would know. Just one quick snip. She wouldn't feel a thing. Maybe we could accidentally throw food on her. Did you see her new shirt on the bus? Evidently she cares how she looks, so let's really mess her up. You could distract her, and I could do it. Tomorrow, it is tomorrow. Today, I looked for her all over the park. Percy told me that she wanted to hike up the mountain, alone. She only thinks about herself. Her so-called husband can't help her now."

Martha's voce drifted downward as though a mini microphone were somehow attached to the vent. The other muffled voice confused me. I didn't know who it was. Was this the way Martha was planning to retaliate with a food fight? I taught middle school for too many years. Wouldn't it be easier just to fight hand-to-hand combat? From now on my hair would be tucked under my pink faded baseball cap. What was good for my ears would be good for hers.

"Leon, I am concerned about that lady that I told you about. I just found out that she wants to cut my hair and drop food on me. Martha, the counselor. You can do that? You mean they can take her certificate away from her. Harassment, yes it is definitely harassment. Then you will look into it? You are going to call the tour director and file a complaint?" I stopped. All conversation from the vent ceased. Two could play at this game if that is what it was. Then I really called Leon.

"You heard what? Sara, grown professional people just don't act that way. Are you absolutely sure that you overheard this conversation?"

"Do you think that I would make up something like this?"

"You do have a vivid imagination. Regardless, no demented jealous woman is going to bother you. Give me the number of the lodge. When I hang up, I will call the tour director and find out exactly what is going on. Certainly, he will be able to stop any physical or verbal threats against you or this will be his last tour. Sara if that counselor lays one hand on you in any way I will have her job as well."

Fuming, Leon had a way with words especially when he was angry. Knowing that I was private property insured that there would be no trespassing. Leon's love consumed me.

"Do I need to take the next flight to, where are you again? Montana?"

"No, I can take care of it. My hair will be tucked under and any thrown food will make the old t-shirt that I wear tomorrow look good. Leon, I didn't mean to get you so upset. I just had to tell you."

"Do you remember when I told you not to go on this trip by yourself? Ever since you left my stomach has been churning. There is just something wrong about this trip. If it hadn't been for your mother's prodding, you never would have gone. Never again Sara will you go off by yourself." His words were spoken like a wounded worried warrior. Leon's love would never be controlled.

My appetite quickly left me. Mental gymnastics took over. A skirmish turned into a battle. Tomorrow, our first stop was visiting the site of the Battle of Little Big Horn. It couldn't be more appropriate. My defensive plan needed to be thought out precisely, ready to go. I fell asleep in full battle gear.

THE BATTLE

THE BRIGHT LIGHT PULLED ME out of my stupor. Exhausted, I fought all night long. Waking up before the victory, I never knew what actually happened. A brisk knock interrupted my thoughts. Hesitating, I really didn't want to answer it.

"Sara, it is Mr. Hudson. May I come in and talk to you for a minute?" Mr. Hudson was either furious or scared. I guess I would find out. "Your husband d called me last evening with some startling accusations. As a tour director I have faced numerous problems but never accusations like this. Sara, is there any chance that you maybe just thought that you heard these things? As a fellow writer, I know that sometimes I tend to over think things."

Mr. Hudson was scared. Who wouldn't be after talking with Leon's rage? Even at the university, if a fellow professor crossed Leon he would make them cry and fall apart like a flakey buttered biscuit. One time he even sent the Dean to the hospital with chest pains and irregular breathing. The dean never crossed him again. I wondered if Leon shared that privy information with Mr. Hudson. Curious, I wanted to ask him, but I didn't. Pale and nervous, Mr. Hudson gazed uncomfortably around the room.

"I apologize if my husband worried you but I heard what I heard." Mr. Hudson readjusted one of his hearing aids. How could he possibly take me seriously when he couldn't even hear what I was saying?

"You know, Sara, my room doesn't even have a heating vent. I don't question whether you heard voices but a threatening conversation? Would anyone in their right mind loudly discuss harassing another person that they just met? No one else has approached me with any sorted details. Shuffling his feet, Mr. Hudson hesitated. Certainly the couple in the next room would have complained, said something to me. You know this group, if something is wrong they want me to know about it right away. Mr. Hudson lowered his voice. Just so that you know, just before I came down I talked with Martha about this conversation that you heard. Very surprised, very upset she seemed more shocked than I was. Folding his arms across his chest, Mr. Hudson gave it his all. Sara, the mind is a finely tuned instrument, like a violin. Separation, lack of sleep, and eight unaccustomed hours on a bus for six days can loosen the strings.

My heart took Mr. Hudson's side. My mind took mine. Trying to correct the wrong, Mr. Hudson's words churned inside me. Mr. Hudson was too nice too naïve for any of this to make any sense.

"By the way, Sara your hair looks nice in a bun. Maybe you should wear it that way for the remainder of the trip. Oh, and on the bus sit up front like you did yesterday." Smiling weakly, Mr. Hudson excused himself and left. Directing a tour was Mr. Hudson's job, not psychoanalyzing his guests. Leon wouldn't bother him again.

I didn't ask for the extra attention. I didn't want the extra attention. But until I shook Mr. Hudson's hand and thanked him for the tour, my guard wouldn't be compromised.

With Mr. Hudson's good intentions, I wondered if Martha's bullying had softened. During breakfast, sleepy tongues probably waged in disbelief and resentment. Older tourists didn't like surprises. A food fight on a crowded bus was beyond their wildest imagination. A trip was an escape from everyday reality, everyday worries. Enjoyment was all they expected.

If I could just concentrate on my plan, the day would take care of itself. I wasn't off to a good start. While talking with Mr. Hudson, the luggage cry had sounded. My bag wasn't ready so I had to haul it down to the bus by myself. It was oddly quiet in the hallway as I dragged my suitcase behind me. I was one of the last ones to make it down to the bus. Everyone just stared blankly as I tried to position my suitcase among the others. No one tried to even help me. My fate was sealed. It had already started. Oddly, the front seat was very empty. A posted sign must have read out of bounds. Actually, I was glad that I didn't have to offer any explanation to anyone about anything. Sitting across from me, Mr. Hudson was engrossed in paper work and looked blankly at me probably wishing that I never set foot on his bus. Both of my feet were planted firmly and were not going anywhere.

The whispers started. "Where is her hair? Did she already cut it off?" It would be much too obvious if I turned around. No one was going to get that satisfaction. Glancing at Mr. Hudson, he didn't hear a thing. If I could just control what I heard. Adjusting my headphones, Bach's melodious harmonies quieted me until I was interrupted with the voice, the unknown voice.

"Sara, do you mind if I sit down?" My instinct roared yes. My mouth answered no. It was Meg. It was a setup. The dead giveaway was the way that she said my name. It was the same as last night. Both my rivals were now known.

"You look so different without your ponytail. I imagine it is cooler without your hair trailing down your back. Dressing down today? No polo shirt? I guess it really doesn't matter what you wear on the bus, does it? Look at me I have worn the same black outfit for days. I just keep washing it out. When I left, I didn't pack much of anything."

Bait, purely bait, and I wanted so much to react to it. I didn't budge. I never noticed Meg's black clothing before. I should have. A silent alarm sounded. Why did I ever start a conversation with her? Her heavy makeup, her clothes, her questions, why didn't I notice these things? I noticed them now. Trying to save souls was one thing, this was another. Meg's face changed before my very eyes. Deception poured out of her.

"I have been so worried since I haven't been able to contact my boyfriend. You know, the one in Finland." This line probably was rehearsed more than once. A convincing actress, Meg should definitely reconsider her profession. Meg's words were drowned out with Mr. Hudson's introduction on the Battle of Little Bighorn. Today I hoped he talked for at least an hour. This was his shortest speech yet.

"Custer's Last Stand is also known as the Battle of Little Bighorn. You have all heard of Crazy Horse and Sitting Bull who were the prominent leaders in this fierce battle between the U.S. Seventh Calvary and the Lakota, Cheyenne, and Arapaho Indian tribes. The battle's famous name originates from its location, which was near the Little Bighorn River in Big Horn County in Montana. It all happened on June 25 and 26 in 1876. George Custer led most of the seven hundred soldiers to their impending death. Custer and two of his brothers were killed. It was considered a victory for the Indians. The Indians didn't want to be confined to their reservations. Once the land belonged to them, they owned it. Infantry and cavalry were unsuccessful in pushing the Indians back into their reservations.

"For all you military history enthusiasts, just after the American Civil War the Seventh Calvary, a veteran organization was formed. Some of the men served in the south, but some had no combat training at all. Immigrants from Germany, Ireland, and England also joined the group.

"You have to remember that this battle was fought on horses, in pen fields, with Indian scouts who couldn't count. That expression 'too many cooks spoil the broth' might apply here. There was little communication between Major Reno, Captain Benteen, and Custer. Numbers deceived. When we get to the battlefield memorial you will be able to read more about the individual battles and the strategies that the commanders used. The Indians outlasted the white men as it were. Violence catered injustice. After viewing all the facts, you decide."

As Mr. Hudson talked, Meg tossed her hair to one side and the other completely uninterested. It didn't really surprise me. In fact, Meg actually seemed rather irritated that Mr. Hudson had interrupted her.

"Battles really don't interest me all that much." Meg yawned. Almost choking, I felt her words stick in my throat. "Anyway it is just another stop to me, something to see, something to read."

Her negative energy cut into me as powerful as any blade. Indifference spewed out of her. Her robust laughter, her openness, her friendliness evaporated. The Meg I met was gone. Avoiding her was all that I wanted to do.

"I am sure that you will reach your boyfriend." I offered, not at all sure nor did I care. My words were chosen carefully without sounding insincere. "Does he travel a lot?"

"Well, he does. He is in the digital business selling computers and other gadgets throughout Europe."

"Did you meet him on a trip?" Instinctively, I knew Meg just needed to focus on herself.

"Actually I did. Did you meet your husband at the college?"

Suddenly I realized that Meg knew way too much about me. Her trusting smile lured me in like a flashy fish line. My mind reeled backwards. Had I really told her everything? Where I worked, what I did, what I just finished. I needed to know what she knew.

"We did meet at college. It was completely random as it often is I guess."

"You mentioned that your husband retired because of health issues. Is that why he didn't come with you on the trip?"

Kicking myself, I wished I never mentioned Leon. Once at dinner, I remembered that I told Meg about Leon's heart attack and how I almost lost him. Did I even reveal the bitterness regarding Leon's prosthesis? Meg worked in a veteran's hospital and knew all about disfigurement. We talked about it. After only one glass of wine, I was painfully transparent. Without wine, I was painfully transparent. Transparent or not, Leon wasn't going to be part of their plan. Thousands of miles would continue to separate him from any hatred.

"The trip just fell at the wrong time. You know how that goes. As it turned out this was a last-minute decision even for me."

Details no longer spewed out of my mouth. Meg noticed. It was no longer about the scenery. It never was.

"I guess I will return to my seat. I have seen all that I need to see. Enjoy the view. You must be thirsty. Here is an extra bottle of water."

The sides of the bottle were misty, slightly chilled. The bottle cap had been slightly twisted open. My thirst wanted to open it, my mind didn't. Could I be taking this too far? I didn't know. I didn't care. I needed to be ready for anything. Reflecting, my armor glistened in the sun.

Setting foot on hardened soil, a real battlefield, I was pushed back in time. There were numerous plaques positioned every hundred feet, giving facts about the gruesome battles. Climbing up a ridge, I could almost smell the war; the ragged limbs torn savagely from their worn-out bodies. Outlines of trees still encircled the field with horses' footprints steeped faintly in the blackened earth. It was surreal to imagine battles with horses and rifled mounted soldiers with bare back tomahawk-laden Indians obsessed with human scalps.

"Sara, was justice done?" Of all the people to ask me that question, it was one of the well-dressed African American men that I casually greeted on the bus. I knew that whatever I said would be closely listened to.

"Just picturing the battles in my mind, I was focused on the physical components of the warfare. It just seems so crude to me. All of it. The Indians just wanted freedom and fought back the only way they could. There was no understanding, no compassion, no compromise."

"Sara, that is war. But was there any justice? My students would probably say yes. Justice at any cost."

Another teacher! I couldn't believe my ears. Was this trip ear marked for school employees? He didn't sound like a teacher, act like a teacher, or look like a teacher. "So you are a teacher?"

"In one way or another, we are all teachers aren't we? But more specifically I am a professor of history. Mr. James, my students call me."

I could have hugged him. An intellect. Leon must have sent him. Professors sounded secure, sounded like they knew what they were talking about even if they didn't. Mr. James's persona embraced me. I relaxed, my defenses were no longer on high alert.

"We have all faced injustice one way or another. People are basically selfish and often don't care how they treat one another. It can happen anywhere, anytime. Sara, it takes at least two for a dispute. Sometimes you can ignore it. Sometimes you can't. People suffer for different reasons, for truth, for dignity, for self-preservation. When you are alone, it is harder to fight."

Pausing, Mr. James nudged the dirt with his tan leather boot. Kindness seeped through his words. This was no longer about Custard's Last Stand. This was no longer about prejudice. This was about me.

"If you were one of my students, you would confide in me. But I will confide in you. Sometimes individuals can't control the anger, the rage, the jealously. You have to understand it, diffuse it or it will devour you." Mr. James stopped shuffling his feet in the colored earth. "Each one of us has a weakness that can destroy us. For me it is the way people look right through me as though I weren't there and don't acknowledge what I do because they don't have to. Pride, jealousy, or love can also break a person. You have to know your weakness so it won't be used against you." My arm reached out to Mr. James. His words were catered for my ears.

"Mr. James I am a fighter. For fourteen years, my husband has trained me to consider options and figure things out for myself. Your historical insight about this battle and other battles has helped me. Your students are lucky to have you as a professor, a mentor, and a friend."

"Sara, I am also a fighter. If you need any support let me know. My wife and I are very good listeners." I cringed at the word. All I needed was another irate wife hating me. "You just blushed. Actually my wife suggested that I talk with you. She knows that I am a problem solver. Traveling alone can be unnerving. I hope another week on this bus is worth it. Not everyone finishes every trip. That might be something for you to consider."

"My mother strongly encouraged me to see my own country before returning to Europe. This is my country."

"Mothers are usually right. Certainly your mother only wants the best for you." With that said, Mr. James carefully maneuvered his way along the ridge joining his waiting wife.

Keenly aware that now everyone on the tour knew everything, I felt even more alienated. Shrugging off the awareness, I headed towards the middle of the field. The spirited eyes on the metal statue of the battle's heroine fastened on to me as I moved down the mound. Realistic or not, it was just a statue. Tourist grabbers surrounded the battlefield's entrance.

Perched like a proud, almost extinct bald eagle, I saw him at a table surrounded by books. His long black braids hung down past his shoulders. His weathered, aged skin sagged slightly on his high cheekbones. By blood he was a Cherokee Indian chief, by profession a professor with a doctorate, and by passion an author. Hovered around him were interested onlookers with insistent questions. I had questions of my own. I waited my turn. Turning towards me, he casually put a book into my empty hands. The back cover portrayed a much younger version of the educated warrior. Age had unearthed tiny crevices into his chiseled face. Dr. Camacho listened intently as he diplomatically answered the white man's doubts. He championed the rights of his people who were now saddled on reservations, poisoning themselves with alcohol and apathy. Abuse eroded their families, stripping their ancestral pride. Dr. Camacho's passion insisted that the younger warriors be college educated, giving every one of them an opportunity to succeed on and off the reservations. Knowledge wouldn't be taken from them. His son who was jabbering on a cell phone at an adjoining table looked nothing like his father, no braids, no cheekbones, no intensity. His genetic warrior gene had vanished.

Dr. Camacho knew there was no returning to the past. Idleness replaced cherished customs. His book witnessed it. Once again unsettled battles surged in my mind. Purchasing the book was the very least that I could do for the challenged tribe. It would compliment Leon's library. The throngs of the crowd nudged me along. Delighted faces and voices passed me. Then I heard more than I wanted to hear.

"Did you see her at that table, spending all that time talking with that author? You would think that she was an author herself."

"Oh didn't you know? She just finished writing her own book."

"You have got to be kidding. Sara wrote a book? Does everyone know that? She never said anything about it when we introduced ourselves and what we did for a living.

"No she didn't. You're the only one who didn't know." That must be why Mr. Hudson tolerates Sara being late sometimes back to the bus. The rest of us can't even be one minute late. So much for equality. Authors have a tendency to get lost in what they are doing. Time doesn't apply to them. If it were anyone else, Mr. Hudson would have kicked her off the bus by now. I even heard that he went up to her room to talk to her."

"Personally, I don't think Sara is at all interesting. In fact, she is rather unassuming and just blends into the background. She acts younger than she is."

"Men must like that. They all want to talk to her."

Then everything faded, the voices got softer and softer. Then there was nothing. Looking around there wasn't anyone from the tour. But the conversation. Who would say these things except for someone who knew me. It just didn't make any sense. The more I thought, then it all made perfect sense.

The assault had begun. It was a tape recording. Somehow Martha had bribed an innocent bystander to walk near me, play the tape, and completely ignore me. It was brilliant but why didn't she just do it herself? My own thoughts were unnerving. Paranoia was not familiar to me. Maybe that was Martha's revised plan, for me to self-destruct without her doing anything. I stopped it. There was a logical explanation for what just happened. It would reveal itself.

Concentrating on what surrounded me, I couldn't help but notice Southwestern artwork in every nook and cranny. Freshly painted murals depicted forgotten lives, families struggling to make a living. I lost myself in their toil. My pleasant afternoon was unexpected. There was no flying food hurled at me from any direction. Not one hair from underneath my cap was disturbed. Maybe Mr. James had derailed the deranged plan just by talking to me. I didn't know. I did know that I had passed a mental test. My polished armor still glistened in the setting sun.

THE AFTERMATH

I COULD HEAR LEON'S MIND at work regarding our last conversation and what he was planning to do. Sara's last conversation clung to Leon. Her every word, played over and over continually in his mind like a deranged tape. His every urge told him to take the very next flight out to South Dakota, locate the demented bus, and end the charade. Forfeiting prepaid monies didn't matter to Leon, his wife's safety did. Sara would never make another week on that bus by herself. Mr. Hudson, the well-meaning tour director assured him that Sara's safety and well being would not be an issue. In fact, he guaranteed Leon that. But how could he? He didn't know Sara. Mr. Hudson was completely unaware of how much confidence Sara didn't have. Outwardly, Sara shouted boldness. Inwardly, Sara whispered insecurity, especially around strangers.

Like hawks to prey, problems attracted Sara. Compassion for others sometimes worked against her convictions. Wanting to help in the worst way, Sara often got herself too immersed. Unselfish waters enveloped her, pulling her out of safety's range. Individuals could be mean, brutal. Growing up in the barrio, Leon knew struggle, knew how to fight. Sara wasn't a fighter, even though he had insisted she become one.

Leon couldn't sit a minute more. He had to do something. Initially, he thought of calling Sara's parents but then thought better of it. Nora would notify the State National Guard or Guards and insist that Herold, her elderly husband, hire a helicopter rescuing Sara in person. Way too much drama, there had to be a better way.

Having a significant rapport with others, Leon knew he would be more effective. Teaching teachers, he knew instincts. He knew how to locate privy information. Background information on these women was going to be essential. Leon had their names, where they lived, and what they did for a living. The rest he would figure out. Martha was easy. A counselor, her contract could be easily pulled for harassment. Meg, a government employee, would have a record, some type of background check, employment history, any ups or downs, firings, any employee disgruntlement. Accessing it would just take persistence. What mattered was who you knew and what they knew. Through his public service, Leon knew many people who were involved in many different walks of life. Most records could be found if you knew entry words and codes. Veteran hospitals were public record, and Leon just happened to know some influential board members. Leon had served on the board of a public access committee supporting the rights of the handicapped. Often members of one committee served on multiple boards of various organizations. Within minutes Leon had access to Meg's file and found some disturbing information. More than once, Meg had been reassigned for her inability to get along with others. She was smart, capable, but unpredictable. Meg was red flagged. Leon didn't need to know anything more. It was already more than enough. It started to make sense. Sara had befriended Meg, who probably twisted and turned her motives endearing herself to his unsuspecting wife––of all the people on the bus to become acquainted with. Leon ached for his wife. Seemingly, Sara's innocence again entangled her. If Meg and Martha were allies, the two of them might be threatening. Jealousy and anger easily held hands.

The phone interrupted Leon's fears.

"Leon, nothing happened. I am fine. I made it through the day without any mishaps. Can you believe it? No thrown food, no hair cut, no nothing. In fact I had a pleasant day, and even bought you a book about real struggles, an Indian's tribe's fight for recognition. My heightened concern was all for not."

"No, Sara you were right to be concerned. I just located some information about Meg and it isn't pleasant."

"Let me guess. Meg is wanted for a parole violation for missing her scheduled counseling appointment since she is out of pocket on a trip."

"Sara, how can you be so casually carefree when just yesterday you were intensely worried? Stay away from Meg. She is unstable."

"What exactly do you mean by unstable? Clinically unstable? Is that what you are referring?"

"No, well, I don't really know. What I do know is that Meg doesn't remain long at any given position."

"That makes her unstable? Maybe she just hasn't found her niche yet."

"Sara, she is over forty. You don't need to know the particulars. Just put distance between yourselves. No more dining out with her, or with Martha for that matter just because it is a novelty. Wait until you get back home and then I will take you out to dinner anytime, anywhere.

"I don't go out to dinner with them anymore. The last time that we all went out together, they both assumed that I was paying since I suggested it. I wasn't and didn't. When the check came, both of them automatically went to the restroom as if on cue. So I told the waiter to readjust the ticket and separate the dinners putting them on individual checks. When returning to the table, their two surprised faces cringed with displeasure. After-dinner mints were almost dislodged in their throats."

"That is exactly what I mean. Don't give them any leverage. Just stay with the group, Sara. Your prearranged dinners have already been paid for. Don't venture out to other restaurants when you don't have to. Eat the food you have paid for. Sara, is it really important for you to finish the trip? I mean would you really miss that much if you didn't?"

"That isn't even a fair question. You know how much I want to explore the National Parks. The Grand Canyon is the very last scheduled park. How could I possible miss that? It is world renown. Everything will be fine. I just know it."

"Your famous last words. This time I guess I just have to trust your judgment, don't I? If anything were to happen, Sara, not only would I have to face my own lack of judgment, but I would have to face your parents' wrath. That is not something that I want to do, especially your mother's wrath. She would never forgive me if anything happened to you."

"Nothing will. Not to change the subject, but you will never guess who I met today. A professor is on this tour. Can you believe it? He talked just like you, very verbal, eager to be understood. So you see that I am trying to mingle with the others."

"Sara, I don't really care if you mingle with the others or not. Just be careful, enjoy the eight-hour bus rides, keep your camera clicking, avoid carry-out food, and tuck your hair under your pink-faded cap. Clothes can be cleaned, but hair takes time to grow."

"You do like my long hair. I always knew it even though you urged me to cut it. We are headed for Mount Rushmore, in South Dakota, where the much-talked-about granite carved busts of the four presidents await us."

"Sara, there is another call. I can't wait to hear all about those busts. Call me if you need me. Behave."

Leon's thought process was pretty much what I envisioned. Leon's love molded everything back into place.

Invigorated, I couldn't wait to explore Mount Rushmore, the granite carvings. There were walking paths that led right next to the cliffs where you could see the enlarged details of each president's face. Mr. Hudson had just passed out pamphlets about the memorial. Looking a little tired, Mr. Hudson encouraged us to discover the park's history by reading on our own. I didn't have to. Listening to the learned voice behind me, I recognized Mr. James vernacular and heard his encouraging wife. Mrs. James wanted to know all about the historical background regarding the memorial.

"The mountain originally had an Indian name, Six Grandfathers. During this time, Tribal Lakota leader Black Elk took a spiritual journey on the mountain. The treaty of Fort Laramie in 1868 gave the Black Hills to the Lakota Indians. However in 1877, the United States took control of the region. In 1885, on a prospecting expedition, the area was renamed Mount Rushmore, after Charles Rushmore who headed up the mission. Someone had the idea of carving famous people into the Black Hills to promote tourism. In 1927, federal funding was given due to efforts of a congressional delegation headed up by President Calvin Coolidge.

"The memorial was first sculpted by Gutzon Borglum and finished by his son, and workers. By 1941, the memorial was completed. Busts of George Washington, Thomas Jefferson, Theodore Roosevelt, and Abraham Lincoln were seen. These four presidents served in the first

150 years of our republic and its expanding territories." Sara knew Mr. James taught history but was surprised how much he knew about the memorial. Genetic, naturally brilliant just like Leon she surmised. "Each head is sixty feet and the entire memorial is 5,725 feet above sea level. The National Park Service services it."

"Just think that we are one of the millions of people that visit the memorial every year," Mrs. James quipped, intrigued with her husband's recall.

"What lies behind the sculptures is equally as intriguing. A chamber was constructed, which contains a vault and sixteen porcelain panels." Sara listened more attentively. "On the panels are inscriptions of the Declaration of Independence, the Constitution, biographies of the four presidents, and historical notes on the United States." It sounded so covert. Sara had to see this chamber.

"Someone, however, had to pay a price, and again it was the Indians. The Indians' rights were abused. And in 1971, the Indians rebelled and occupied Mount Rushmore renaming it Mount Crazy Horse. A prayer staff was erected on top of the mountain and a shroud covered the president's faces. The antagonism was never really resolved. The Indians realized that they couldn't have Mount Rushmore, so they built their own monument honoring Crazy Horse. The irony of all this is that Gutzon Borglum, who initially carved the faces representing justice, truth, equality, and everything honorable, was a member of the Ku Klux Klan. How's that for equality?"

"It wasn't. It doesn't surprise me at all that our government hired someone like that."

I wasn't the only one listening. An agitated gentlemen a few seats back stood up and wouldn't sit down. "We should boycott the memorial and just go to Crazy Horse's monument. I would rather support the Indians than a racist foundation." It got really quiet on the bus. Mr. James slowly stood up and turned around even slower.

"You don't have any idea of what racism is. You need to sit down and keep your comments to yourself. If you personally don't want to support this outing, don't. This isn't about you. It is about forty other people who want to see Mount Rushmore and not be ignorant about its conception."

This was riot material. Mr. and Mrs. James were one of the few African Americans on the bus. But he was the only professor on the bus, and everyone knew it. Mr. Hudson didn't say a word but just stared ahead. I wondered if his hearing aids were turned on. Then Mrs. James stood up.

"As my husband said, you have no idea what racism is."

Heat poured out of her words. Mentally, I was already standing. All I had to do was get up. Just as I was about to stand up, Mr. Weeks, an elderly man in his eighties, put his shoulder around the verbal agitator.

"Please come and sit with me and tell me how you feel." The anger melted like butter on a hot piece of roasted corn. The finger pointing stopped. The squirming stopped. Never mind the monument, everyone looked like they wanted to boycott the bus, even the bus driver.

Every couple of minutes, the bus driver, who proudly displayed a Vietnam War Survivor plaque, kept checking his rear view mirror. His face was stoic except his eyes, which combed each aisle, waiting. His eyes stated that there would be no more outbursts on his bus from anyone. Not one more disruption. would be tolerated. His stance mentally dared you to stand up.

Turning around, two bold loving hands were clasped in unity. Wishing that my own bold loving hand had one to clasp, I clutched my fingers tightly, promising never again to think a prejudiced thought. Before long, the bus rolled into a long steep incline leading into Mount Rushmore. I wasn't sure which would have more impact, the drama on the bus or the memorial sculpted by a bigot. Mr. Hudson seemed oblivious to the skirmish. Maybe there was a pre-arranged pact that gave the bus driver authority to dispel any disruptions.

Off the bus, everyone scattered like homing pigeons. No one waited for anyone. Tours led by young, eager, microphone-clad rangers were available. No one went near them. One disturbing fact was enough. Colorful flags from every state lined the entryway and washed away the bus's prejudice, filling me with pride. Our nation was such a young nation with so many skirmishes between so many different nationalities. Gazing at the presidents, it was surprising that the republic survived at all. Mounted high-powered binoculars were positioned on the many tiered bleachers, ready to zoom in for a closer look. The facial details were so life-like as though any moment any one of the presidents would rise ready to answer any question.

I gulped in patriotism. Four-piece musical quartets had musicians clad in red, white, and blue. National anthems and early spirited songs of the republic sang out, reminding me of the contests in elementary school when we tried to feverishly out sing one another. To be an American filled me with overflowing pride. Just to have the opportunity to visit this memorial said it all.

Ant-like tourists from all over the world scurried everywhere. It was an international showcase. Amazed faces peered out from under caps and shawls. This was my country that enthralled them. Bits of Chinese, Japanese, Korean, French, German and other linguistic flavors perked up my ears. It reminded me of Europe where ethnicity meshed momentarily then went its separate way. Surprisingly, hiking boots were the footwear of choice even though it was one hundred degrees. The cliff, rocky incline, and large boulders advertised difficulty. My sneakers knew rocky soil. You just had to be aware of where you stepped and what you stepped on. Being from New England, I knew.

It was further than I thought from the bleachers to the cliff-face. Without water, it made it even longer. Everyone toted a bottle of water except for me. The water-lines formed an endless maze, so I didn't even bother. Water didn't seem that important until now. Half way up, I perched on a big glistening granite boulder, getting a hawk's eye view of the terrain. The rock's mica whirled me back into childhood when my father's favorite outing took us into huge rock quarries hunting for mica and quartz crystals. This rock would have been a prize.

Sitting off to the side of the well-trodden path, I quietly reflected on the sculpture. Visualizing the four hundred workers, I imagined the ropes, pulleys, and trolleys that took them to the very top of the mountain. I didn't remember hearing anything about accidents or casualties, but with blasting dynamite there must have been some. Why would anyone jeopardize their safety to such a degree? It was that pioneer spirit. That insistence knowing that you could do anything. I had a cliff to climb.

"Are you alright?" A friendly face persisted. "Your face is beet red. I just happen to have an extra bottle of water. Here take it." Before I even had the chance to thank him, it was thrust into my hand. "This is South Dakota. In this heat, you are defeated without some kind of liquid. It is your heart, your blood pressure that you need to be concerned about, never mind your aching legs." The persistent voice concealed a Swiss accent. Somewhat of a novelty, he was clad in hiking britches and knee highs. Rugged and good looking, he shouldn't have been alone. But no little Swiss Miss trailing behind him ever appeared. "Can I help you off that rock?" A gentlemen. The water tasted even better.

"No, I am fine. I can make it."

"Would you mind someone hiking with you? Anything can happen on a cliff. I am Stofard." He grinned confidently. No one ever refused him before; I was certain of it. Why should I ruin his record? I didn't. His question just caught me off guard. I just assumed that he would continue toting his extra water bottles up the mountain aiding innocent victims along the way.

"Well, why not. It's Sara. Have you heard about the chamber behind the faces?" With that said, words that weren't there just started tumbling out of my mouth. Stofard sprinkled his English with bits of Swiss-French. Once again, I was in the Swiss Alps on that rocking chairlift listening to cowbells clanging beneath me. The trail arched just below the faces. There was an obscure sign pointing towards the back of the mountain for further climbing. Maybe the chamber was open only during certain times of the year. But this was the middle of summer. It just didn't make any sense.

"Not much of a sign was it? Where did you hear about this chamber? Are you sure it is back in this direction?" Not going into any of the biased details, I explained to Stofard what the chamber was supposed to contain. Assuring him that we were headed for the right direction, he couldn't wait to see the historical panels, the fundamental truths of our nation. Hiking briskly, my footwork was a mantra as my eyes followed what was ahead of me. Two energized healthy legs extended from a well-developed torso moved easily. It was odd for me to actually be hiking with someone since Leon was handicapped and walked with difficulty. Glimpses of what could have been dangled in front of me. Had I settled for enough? It was just so nice to share the outdoors with someone who could move.

Stofard probably was selfish, way too independent, and unable to change like me. After all, he was traveling by himself, again like me. Maybe it meant something. I didn't know. Enjoying the view, I almost missed the chamber. Stofard walked right by it. It was off to the right below the path. No one entered or exited. Being quite a ways past the sculpture, my own legs felt detached. As we entered the chamber, I don't know why but I expected to be met by a welcoming soldier passing out historical memorabilia. No uniform revealed itself. Ceiling vaults with sun-lit recesses allowed you to examine the documented panels. Stofard was in a trance.

"Sara, being a rock climber, I am curious about obscure, out-of-the-way passages. This chamber just might have a secret vault or two." The trance was broken. Visions of amputated appendages popped into my mind. Watching too many documentaries on entangled rock climbers, I knew now why Stofard was alone. Crouching into an enclosed algae-laden tunnel was not one of my favorite pastimes. It breathed claustrophobia. Stofard halted. The sign read not responsible for lost items. Did that include hands and feet? Stofard had already vanished down the narrow gap. That's when I heard it. The dreaded words.

"Sara, over here, somehow my foot got snagged in this crevice." Pretending not to hear, I tried to block out his words. It was no use. His cry echoed down the chamber's wall over and over again. Did Stofard really expect me to dislodge his foot? Unfamiliar with dislodging techniques, I envisioned the worst possible scenario, the dreaded cut. Why was I so insistent on seeing this chamber? More than anything I wished that I had never rested on that boulder. Who would go for help? What if that took hours? What if the bus left without me? How would I ever get home? How would I ever explain this? My selfishness drowned out my empathy. Stofard must have heard because he looked guilty.

"It's not as bad as it looks, Sara. I just needed an extra pair of hands. Let me tell you what to do." Being a teacher, I could follow directions as well as give them and did what I was told.

"You did it. It wiggles. It's free. Cramped unlit spaces can be dangerous. I guess that is part of the attraction. You never know what is going to happen. Sorry if I concerned you."

Concerned was that all that Stofard could say. I didn't want to hear another word. It was enough and didn't matter. What only mattered was fresh air.

"I am going back. Enjoy your cramped tunneling."

"I am right behind you. Lead the way."

The hot, muggy air stirred slightly as I breathed in a mouthful. No longer was I visually impaired. Stofard's intrigue was a liability. I couldn't wait to get away from him and his traumatized foot.

"Are you able to get down the mountain?"

"Sara, I am so sorry if I scared you. Adventure is just in my blood."

"It is not in mine. The most adventurous thing that I have ever done is to go on this trip without my husband."

"Your husband, you have a husband? You never mentioned him."

"No, I never did. But if he were with me, I guess I wouldn't be resting alone on granite boulders. The problem is that he can't climb cliffs and that is why he isn't here.

"I just assumed that...I thought that we might even be able to celebrate my newfound freedom, my foot freedom that is."

I suddenly remembered why I didn't enjoy conversations with Swiss men even when I was in Switzerland. They couldn't see beyond their Swiss accents. Miraculously, Stofard's foot started to move in unison with his other foot. Before I knew it, we were below the presidents, headed down.

"Stofard, there you are." It was cliff-descending music to my ears. I was relieved of my duty to the injured man.

"Sara, this is Martre. She also is not a cliff climber."

"Stofard, what happened to your foot?"

My smile just got bigger and bigger and bigger. I did no better on this mountain than off this mountain. I didn't care. Wanting to get off this mountain by myself, I did. Before I knew it, Stofard and Marte were merely relieved Swiss accents trailing way behind me.

At the bottom of the mountain, other different savory accents greeted me as I walked through the tired crowds tasting food at the individual booths. Finding a table, I munched on sweet potato fries while listening to varied musical flavors of tribal instruments. A musical Cherokee family who recorded their own CDs was performing next to me. It was so unusual because they were of mixed heritage. The wife was white, very pale and shy, evidently the manager of the group. Her husband was full Cherokee and every inch of him was musical. He played many classical instruments and ones akin to his tribe, especially the wooden flute and the hanging washboard. My ears danced in delight, mesmerized. Each family member soloed their expertise on the trumpet, violin, flute, and base drums. I watched as the wife artfully readjusted the sound system and wondered what it would be like married to a touring, musical Native American. That would be an adventure. The wind-swept sounds healed my trying afternoon.

The twilight ceremony at the Mount Rushmore Memorial couldn't be missed. Surprisingly, it was Meg who convinced me to go. Maybe that musical phrase, "What a difference a day makes," applied here. Friendly and interested, Meg was no longer Martha's pitch woman. In fact, she confided in me how Martha had slighted her. Listening, I was so relieved that there was no Swiss accent. As the streaked sun tumbled into the horizon, the warmed bleachers grew cold. The stilted speakers blared then a solemn, hushed voice commemorated the honorable serviceman who served in all branches of the armed forces. With colorful lighting, the president's faces turned from hues of red, white, and blue. Fireworks continually exploded filling the air with sulfur mist. This Fourth of July was a novelty, seeing, hearing, smelling, and embracing the passionate patriotism.

But it didn't compare to breathing in the smelly mosquito repellant, jostling for the best seat on the spread-out folded blankets, and inhaling the melted Good Humor ice cream bars that stuck to your fingers. Gazing at the star-studded sky, we waited anxiously for the first spread of fiery color. Those New England Fourth of July family memories could never be outdone.

Without even a hinted rumble, the celebrated skies opened up and rain-soaked arms and legs ran for cover. Meg must melt as she couldn't reach a nearby wooden roof quickly enough. Lingering behind, my sore legs didn't respond. Despite the rain, the cutting words rang out.

"All alone by herself, it just doesn't surprise me. Drenched she looks like a water rat."

"What would you expect?"

There was no time to listen. Hurrying, an elderly lady in front of me almost lost her step. She lit up like an uncovered lamp when I scoped my arm around her shoulder, helping her towards shelter. The voices were chased away by the light.

INDIANS AND PAINTED PONIES

WE WERE INTO THE SECOND week of the trip; and unbelievably, I was still on the bus, much to everyone's surprise, especially Martha. This morning, I couldn't help but notice steam-like mist encircling Martha's ears as I overheard her comment to Mr. Hudson about my dark eye circles and how tired I looked. Maybe I was even ill and needed bed rest. I guess that explained why Mr. Hudson hurried towards me to see for himself. Documentation of course. I told Mr. Hudson that with only four hours of sleep, I was doing pretty well, especially since my mattress felt like a lumpy water bed.

Immediately, Mr. Hudson was much more concerned about my lodging than my health. He casually told me to take it easy and just keep the group insight. Martha casually watched as we talked. Not wanting to disappoint her, I yawned widely, slowly sinking back down in my comfortable chair, having another large cup of coffee. It was now my turn to observe. Irritated that Mr. Hudson did absolutely nothing, Martha got up abruptly and almost fell out of her chair. Not moving an inch, Joel, her stoic husband, didn't seem to care.

Considering Joel, I could understand his misery. His vacation was jolted because his wife was here and maybe he wished she weren't. His body language spoke volumes.

Unannounced, Percy promptly sat down beside me, ordered a cup of tea, and with a glazed look in her eyes couldn't wait to tell me all about Crazy Horse and his monument, today's first destination. A paperback book all about the victorious warrior tumbled out of her side pocket.

"I have been up all night reading about Crazy Horse," Percy proclaimed, wanting everyone to hear.

Her timid nature vanished. "I wish that I had known him, ridden on his pinto horses, and lived in a weathered tepee in his tribe. To be courted by him, to be dragged willingly to his tepee would have been an adventure. If only I could somehow ride a horse back into time."

And I thought I was the one with an imagination. To me, it was whimsical that Percy envisioned herself as an Indian squaw, squatting on a dirt floor, mashing berries for war paint, and cleaning animal hides for her Indian chief. I couldn't wait to hear the rest of it.

"Crazy Horse wasn't born that long ago. Back then, information regarding births and deaths were passed down by word of mouth. There was no records, no city halls, no verification. So sometime between 1840 and 1845, he was born to an Oglala Lakota Indian tribe. At first he was named Cha-O-Ha, which meant 'one with trees in the wilderness.' Just listen to that sound. Much more musical than Percy. His father was named Crazy Horse and when Cha-O-Ha matured, strong and dominant, he was renamed Crazy Horse. Just like we do today, inheriting his father's name. Rattling Blanket Woman was his mother. She probably talked too much. I would have liked her. Unfortunately when he was young, Crazy Horse saw his tribal leader, Conquering Bear, killed. Afterwards, his trance visions began. As you can imagine, his father was beside himself and took him to South Dakota on a vision quest. Supposedly, that would cure him."

"I remember reading that the Indians ate parts of the peyote cactus to induce trances. But it sounds like Crazy Horse had his naturally. I guess a vision quest today would be like a four-week stay at a hospital heavily medicated." My humor wasn't appreciated. Percy didn't even seem to hear me.

"Led by a red-tailed hawk into the Black Hills, father and son communed with nature and the spirits when Crazy Horse had a profound vision, which probably scared his father to death. His vision took Crazy Horse to the South, which represented death in the Indian world. He was brought back and then taken to the spiritual West, where he encountered thunder beings. During his vision, he was mounted on a horse that danced as if a shadow turning in all directions. Some speculate this is where his father renamed him after the dancing of the crazy horse. If you just close your eyes, you can see the two of them dancing in that spiritual world." Maybe Percy would have blended nicely into the tribe after all. "In that vision, Crazy Horse was shown his warrior face paint, which consisted of a yellow lightning bolt with hailstones made with white powder. In battle, there would be no eagle feathered war bonnet on his head like most of the other warriors. Crazy Horse was told that he would be a protector of his people." I was so thankful that I didn't have visions. Dealing with individuals in this world was difficult enough without seeing and conversing with people who weren't really there.

"After the vision, Crazy Horse received much power. During battle, he had the ability to put himself back into the spiritual world, protecting himself. A medicine man gave Crazy Horse a black stone to protect his black-and-white-painted horse. The pair was never injured during many battles between the Crow, Shoshone, Pawnee, and Blackfeet Indians."

"There were so many Indian tribes that didn't get along. Land, property, and human rights were an issue just like it is today. How sad that nothing has really changed." I added.

Percy nodded. "You are right. Even on this bus some people just don't seem to want to get along with others."

Later at the monument when I looked Crazy Horse in the eye, I would probably envision his crazy, spotted horse dancing as he held on for dear life, clutching the black stone as the sunlight lit up his facial lightning bolt. Illuminated, Percy continued.

"There were also many battles with the white man. Remember how Crazy Horse was involved at the battle of Little Bighorn? Well in 1877, there was a plan to capture Crazy Horse, arrest him, and take him to the white man's headquarters. Once captured, Crazy Horse refused to submit and died in defiance. He lived and died a hero, a symbol of victory." Reliving it, a grieving look crossed Percy's face. A long, quiet minute passed.

"Percy, don't you think that Crazy Horse would be honored to know that the white man has written books about him?"

"Maybe he would. Maybe he wouldn't. At the monument, Crazy Horse points toward the Black Hills and the plaque he stands on reads, 'My lands are where my dead lie buried.' He knew what belonged to him."

"Considering all of the battles that occurred, if nothing else, Crazy Horse did get recognition. I saw on the map that there are two highways named after Crazy Horse. One of them is the Crazy Horse Memorial Highway, which leads to the memorial. In a way, he did get his lands."

"Sara, it is just so unfortunate that the Indians had such a difficult time keeping what was rightfully theirs. If it wasn't one of their own, it was the white man ripping apart their possessions."

"Percy, it was never acceptable. There are lessons to be learned. Each one of us has the ability to poison and destroy, or to understand and allow." A book about an honorable warrior can be seductive. Percy just needed an intriguing boyfriend.

Within fifteen minutes we were packed, saddled, and cruising down Crazy Horse Memorial Highway. Mr. Hudson attempted to send us back to the seventies as he entertained us with an outdated Lucielle Ball comedy video. There were just so many tricks to break up a two-hour highway ride. This one worked. The video reminded me of the foolish things that Leon and I argued about, little things that amounted to nothing. Two weeks seemed like an eternity. My priorities were realigned. Nature and beauty were one thing. Leon was quite another. My selfishness would no longer sit directly beside me. When I returned, my dusted-off love would be noticed. Last night, the Black Hills once again prevented me from talking to Leon. There was so much to reveal: Mount Rushmore, the patriotic speeches, the fireworks, and Stofard. Well, maybe not Stofard. He would remain an annoying Swedish memory.

Immense, Crazy Horse's monument looked every bit a protector, might and victory embodied in stone. Even unfinished, the statue's pride was not diminished. It was humbling facing Crazy horse without an army. Near the statue, there was an unsettling uneasiness. No one from any of the other tour groups seemed to want to spend much time alone at the monument, except Percy who couldn't take her eyes off her warrior. Maybe some of the white man's guilt was unearthed, uncovered, and examined. It would be shameful not to honor the statue's completion. Spontaneous, pocket donations along with admittance fees would help fuel the needed work.

"Would you mind taking our picture with Crazy Horse?" a patient voice asked hidden under a big floppy hat. Toting a heavy knapsack with protruding camera lenses, Kito the Japanese man handed me a loaded camera with numerous additional gadgets. "Don't be intimidated with the lenses. Just keep the two of us centered in the rectangle." Quickly appearing at his side, Kito's perky wife permitted him to remove his hat for the picture. With one click they were captured alongside Crazy Horse.

"That is quite a camera that you have. I hope that I focused correctly."

"With all of the different lenses, sometimes it is more difficult than others. One of the perks for working for National Geographic Magazine is using the latest, most-up-to-date camera with all of its attachments. This trip has given me a chance to film in detail, focusing on all the earthen colors, the multi-layered erosion carved rocks, and man's personal dedications. This is Margaret, my wife of many happy years. Our anniversary gift to one another is this trip. Growing older together makes bending and reaching more tolerable."

Studying my face, Margaret blurted out, "You also are also very fair. The sun is scorching. Your hat should be bigger." Margaret could have been my mother. It was exactly what she would have said.

"Nature is such an integral part of our lives. Kito takes the pictures and I help crop them, develop them, choosing the best angles getting them ready for production. The magazine is picky, but by now so are we. We have been doing this for twenty years. In fact, the word retiring has been mentioned, but it is just a word. Without our photo shoots, things would be way too quiet.

"It sounds so exciting. How in the world did you get started?"

"Kito took some photos of our favorite migratory birds, the brown pelicans, and submitted them in a photo contest and won. Living in California, we have access to many birds, and to all kinds of wildlife."

"What a wonderful adventure. For me, this is as adventurous as I get. Exploring the national parks is contagious. Hiking and sightseeing in this heat would only attract a certain breed, nature lovers. Most of my family cringed when I told them that I would be riding on a bus numerous hours a day, hiking, and peering at rock displays in the middle of the desert. My husband for one couldn't really grasp the attraction. You are lucky that both of you share your love of nature."

"Winning the bird contest changed our lives completely. Sometimes spontaneity is rewarded. Sometimes it isn't. Once the camera is in my hands, I forget about everything. When the light is right, you have to be ready to move. Once in a while, Margaret has to reposition me for safety reasons. We make a good team. Sara, right now we are ready to move towards that wrapped around porch, the one with the hammocks. It was once a historical residential home that was later turned into a restaurant. Can you smell the lemon, barbecue meat, and envision large goblets of chilled red wine? Around here, it is supposed to be one of the better places to eat, maybe the only place. We would be very pleased if you would join us." Surprised, I couldn't say no. They had already said yes.

In the middle of nowhere, the only needed advertisement was wafting food scents. The restaurant was already jam-packed. Outside, hammocks were full, swinging in anticipation. Bypassing the hammocks, we were ushered in as Kito's big and bulky camera bag caught someone's attention. Kito flashed a few hand signals, and we were escorted to a waiting table. Hurrying, Kito could taste what he wanted, a glass of chilled wine. Already at the table, other couples from our tour greeted us. Some I knew, some I didn't. Mr. and Mrs. James gave me a quick, curious smile. As soon as we sat down, ears and eyes vied for Mr. Hito's attention. He seemed to expect it. Wine was selected while Mr. Hudson quickly joined the assembly, sat down, looking surprised to see me. Was there an age limit for this table? The menu's prices were higher than I expected. A nagging feeling hovered over me when I remembered that my wallet was camouflaged inside my sweater on my bus seat. How could I excuse myself politely and not return? Margaret intervened.

"This is our treat, order whatever you want."

Her words soothed me like a pain killer. Surprised and relieved, I joined in the conversation, toasting to the trip with a raised glass of red wine. Randomly, the topic of published works surfaced in the group. When Mr. Hudson revealed how he compiled information to write his touring book, his whole demeanor changed. The Bonsons not only took photographs but wrote about them. Margaret flushed as she told us about her first published article about migrating hummingbirds that sometimes rested their beating wings, which surprised some of her readers. Not surprised at all, Mr. James had published some historical research in his own field, *History in the Making.* Many professors published, but for Mr. James, research was his passion. Ears opened and eyes widened when I revealed that it took me eight years to write my memoir that was just about to be published. Like popcorn, questions popped. I gushed about Leon and his life, from poverty, to prejudice, his life-altering battle with a drunken driver that took his leg, and his legacy as a beloved professor. Reaching out to Leon, they empathized, wanting to know how he accomplished so much with so little. They couldn't wait to purchase the book. It was a promising response from a random audience. Missing Leon even more, I wished that he could hear their encouragement. The cutting words laced into me.

"She thinks she is the star of the table. I can't believe that someone actually asked her to sit there. She probably invited herself. I doubt if any of the others have anything in common with her. They must feel sorry for her. She doesn't even carry any identification."

My last mouthful of red wine almost toppled out of my mouth. It was midday, and it could be the two glasses of rich, red wine that I just consumed. But it wasn't. No one paused. Crowded, small and enclosed, you couldn't help but hear other engaged voices around you. The negative comments stopped as soon as they started. A flaming peach desert appeared out of nowhere, compliments of Mr. Hudson. It was relished by all and quickly devoured. The fleeting sarcasm wouldn't dim this luncheon. Nothing did.

Mr. Hudson made motions to the bus driver, who was seated a few tables away from us. Glancing quickly, I saw swirls of steamed coffee rising from his mug and was thankful that it wasn't chilled red wine. No one really wanted to leave knowing that there was an awfully long drive ahead of us crossing Wyoming into the Colorado mountains. Mr. Hudson was beside himself. Everyone was visibly upset. Some were angry, some wanted to wait, and some didn't. Percy was missing. The last time that I saw her was at the statue of Crazy horse. I always envisioned myself being terribly late, not someone as organized as Percy. Mr. Hudson's mantra, "Be on time or get left behind," was tested. Anxiously waiting, Mr. Hudson climbed in and out of the bus peering at his watch as if it would disappear. Flying accusations were everywhere. I thought for sure this time a riot on the bus was unstoppable. Then the unthinkable happened. The bus started and stalled. We were not going anywhere. The bus wouldn't start again. I breathed a sigh of relief. I had to find Percy. Somehow I felt somewhat responsible. No one else knew that Percy was crazy about Crazy Horse. That thought never left my mind.

PERCY'S VISION

PERCY COULDN'T TAKE HER EYES off the warrior's cement face. The more she looked, the more she yearned. Light-headed she sat down and an unaccustomed dizziness swept over her. She collapsed. When she opened her eyes, nothing looked even vaguely familiar. There was no bus, no tourists, no statue. There were only rugged tepees in the distance, with roaming horses and buffalos in an open field. It was the photograph from her book.

"I pulled you through." A rugged warrior's face bent down lifting her up. "You wanted my way of life, to live in my tribe, so I allowed you to enter."

Up until now, Percy had never experienced anything in her life that was surreal. This was beyond surreal. Recognizing the yellow lightning bolt, Percy couldn't take her eyes off it.

"Are you...are you Crazy horse?"

"Why yes, who did you expect? Most of the others can't even look directly into my eyes. But your eyes never left my face. And now here you are. You will be happy with us."

Percy was certain that she was hallucinating. Someone must have slipped something into her diet soft drink. Regardless, she was going to enjoy every bit of this delusion.

"The others will take care of you and show you what to do." A long black braid swished by her face as she held onto Crazy horse and the bare back of a painted horse.

Startled, Percy looked down and saw that her clothing was identical to all of the other squaws surrounding her. Staring at her face and pointing to her eyes and lips, the squaws were fascinated with her blue eye makeup and pink lipstick. Introducing herself and listening to the words coming out of her mouth, Percy hesitated. It wasn't English but sounded identical to the words from the book that she had practiced over and over again. The women had silky, braided black hair. The wind tossed Percy's long loose auburn hair. Her reddened hair was the color of kindling fire. Nervously, the squaws stepped backward when a taller Indian lady with colorful facial markings and numerous beads approached Percy. Reaching out her brown hand, she took hold of Percy's right hand. Watching, the others looked as though they had witnessed an apparition. This had to be the tribe's female leader, Crazy Horse's counterpart, Percy hoped.

"I am Rattling Blanket." The book's photograph didn't do her justice. It was Crazy Horses's mother. Percy was in very good hands. "You must be hungry after your long journey."

"You have no idea how long my journey was. I am not from here. I mean I came from another life."

"My son has told me where you come from. It doesn't matter. All that matters is your love for my son."

Percy's face heated up. She never should have confided in Sara. Somehow the whole tribe knew her inner most feelings.

"Eat, there are chores to be done, preparation needs to be made."

The buffalo meat was surprisingly tender, and whatever she drank quenched her thirst. Remembering about the tribe's daily activities, Percy was ready to contribute. The blue and red berries were in separate mashing bowls. Animal hides were over in a corner and needed to be tanned. Rattling Blanket stoked a small fire as numerous squaws brought brightly colored beaded linens into the tepee.

"Try these on. It is for your ceremony." Rattling Blanket quietly urged.

"My ceremony?" What did they have planned? Sickened, Percy realized that she was in trouble. Sara's words clung to her. *"The Indians sacrificed."* A painted horse was blessed by the medicine man. It was an escape. She could ride.

"Your wedding ceremony to my son." Percy couldn't believe her ears. "It is tonight."

Everything in her cringed. The old adage "Be careful what you wish for" pounded in her brain. After all, this is what she wanted, wasn't it?

Percy felt the berry paint drip down her face. She was covered in colors and her hair was braided with lavender scented flowers. The orange sun was setting and all of his beauty stood before her.

His beaded, eagle feathered tunic outlined his brown muscular arms that waited eagerly for the spiritual embrace. Crazy Horse's eyes danced with love. Somehow he loved Percy and longed for her. Dancing in unison, his warriors cried out one by one pushing the couple closer and closer together. In the distance, Percy heard an incessant baying, Crazy Horse's painted pony. The ceremony began. Percy tried in vain to remember from the book about what happened in the wedding ceremonies but couldn't. She wondered where Crazy Horse's other wives were. Suddenly appearing, all five of them bowed slightly towards her. Knives flashed. The blood ritual. Percy remembered. Mutilating her body for love was not something that appealed to her. Her infatuation with Crazy Horse ended then and there. Her wild imagination had gotten her into this, and it would get her out of this. Crazy Horse's pony must have known and edged closer to her, winnowing. Percy smelled the potent sweetness of cactus laced with alcohol as she watched the warriors gulp down the hypnotic liquid. Breaking the circle, Percy jumped on the painted pony's back, digging her heels into its heaving sides. The wind carried them both as Percy's cries reached Sara's ears.

Sara sensed that Percy would be somewhere near the statue. A group of anxious tourists huddled together, covering an unconscious body with sweaters. No one really knew what to do as they carefully elevated her head and legs and placed ice packs on her forehead. The lifeless figure started crying. Sara knew the voice. She had to get to the voice.

"Percy, Percy, where are you? Spying her downed friend Sara called out, "It's Sara. You just had an accident, fell down, and hit your head."

Percy couldn't let Sara in; she needed to protect Sara. Sara had a husband who loved her and expected her to return from this National Park bus trip. But Sara wasn't in love with Crazy Horse. She hardly even listened when she read his biography from the book. To Sara, the Indians were just a part of prejudiced history.

"Percy, you are safe. Don't cry. Just try to relax and slowly open your eyes." Percy heard other voices, whisperings. Only one person at a time could be pulled through. Now, her fear wouldn't bind her eyes. Slowly adjusting, Percy's eyes let in the afternoon light and Sara's drawn face.

"What happened, where am I? The painted pony?"

"Percy, there is no pony."

"But, the others, the ceremony, my face." Sara took Percy's hand, calming her, noticing very faint strains of a blue hue on Percy's cheeks. Something did happen, Sara just wanted the crowd to disperse and get Percy up and moving. Slowly the concerned onlookers left one by one as Sara's determined arms steered Percy to a bench.

"Sara, I don't need this anymore. I don't want this anymore," Percy whispered, handing me the ear marked book on Crazy Horse. "I don't ever want to read about him again. My imagination will no longer rush ahead of me. I can't wait to get back on the bus."

I couldn't even imagine what happened to Percy but that dreamy faraway look was no longer in her eyes. Trying to focus beyond her piercing headache, Percy's sandal-clad feet headed for the bus, grateful that she no longer donned ceremonial Indian dress. Every bit of the humid afternoon was refreshing.

ALPINE VILLAGES
AND ARCHES

LEON'S SUBDUED VOICE SOUNDED VERY distant. More than anything, I wanted to hear his sweetness and reassurance.

"Well, you made it thus far into the second week."

"The parks really haven't overshadowed the daily eight-hour bus rides. I don't remember that particular factor mentioned in the travel brochure's write up. It would have made a difference."

"Sara, you are traveling through numerous states. What do you expect? What state are you in now?"

"We are headed for the mountains in Colorado. You wouldn't believe the monument at Mount Rushmore, the four busty presidents. They were so lifelike. And the brilliant fireworks' display at night dipped them in red, white, and blue. Hiking up the mountain, I saw panoramic, quiet mountains, listened to bristling pine trees, and wondered at the shape and color of multi-layered cliffs. You were right there with me."

"Rocks. I never thought a bus full of strangers could lure you away from me for two weeks to look at carved rocks, mountain rocks, pine trees, and whatever else is out there. All day and all night, the cats cry out for you. My affection isn't enough for them. What has happened to our arranged calling times at night?"

"Leon, some of the lodges have phone service and some don't."

"What about your cell phone? Is that blocked as well?"

"Every time I try to call you, there is no service. It isn't as though I forget."

"Sara, this is not working for me. We have never been away from each other for more than one night. It has been ten nights. I am beginning to feel single again."

"In four days, I will be home. Promising you from now on that trip reservations will be in both of our names or neither of our names."

"It is a relief to hear you say that. Go on, I just know you have something unbelievable to tell me."

"I do, and you really won't believe it. I hardly do. It happened at Crazy Horse's monument. Do you remember Percy, the fashion editor from Las Vegas that I told you about? Well at Crazy Horse's monument, she just disappeared and no one could find her. Before vanishing, all Percy talked about were Indians, in particular Crazy Horse. She purchased a book about him and read almost the whole thing to me. Somehow Percy fell, hit her head, and was unconscious. I found her on the ground in a middle of a throng of strangers. Dazed and disorientated, Percy had a piercing headache, but other than that she was alright."

"Sara, none of this sounds good. Every time I talk to you something bad has happened to you or someone else. Where was Mr. Hudson the competent tour director?"

"Well, the way it works is once we get to a destination, and get off the bus, we are on our own until we regroup later at a designated time. Percy just never showed up."

I wanted to tell Leon about my treated luncheon, the red wine, and fleeting whispering, but I didn't dare. Percy's blue-tinted streaked face still flashed at me with unanswered questions. I would figure it out and tell Leon when I got home.

"Sara, if things don't straighten out, I am going to get that tour director fired one way or the other. The last conversation I had with him on the phone he reassured me that everything was going smoothly. Evidently, it isn't. Just get home in one piece Sara. The cats need to be fed. Call me tomorrow. I don't care if you have to climb over the mountains. Call me." After that implicit instruction, Leon abruptly hung up.

It was one hundred degrees in the middle of July, and the bus was headed for a snowless alpine village. Many years ago, when I was single, I took my vacations during the winter months visiting many of the renowned ski resorts. We were just a few hours away from one of them. Vail was a remote ski village with enticing beauty. From the airport, I remember it took the bus three arduous hours just to get there. I couldn't get my skis on fast enough as newly fallen soft powder clung to the sides of the mountain. After skiing all day, I relaxed in an outside hot tub with a snifter of warm cognac as swirling snowflakes fell around me. My memories lulled me to sleep.

Going up the steep incline, the bus jolted, whined, and puffed smoke. Cringing, I hoped that it didn't break down again and concentrated on what lay outside my window. Without its tuffs of snow, stacked skies, and ice-coated store fronts, the brown sloping earth with lofty green tree tops looked oddly out of place. Huddled together at the bottom of the mountain were numerous shops that sported high-end clothes, accessories, and whatever else you could imagine. A fast moving rippled stream etched itself through the village. It was a still picture from a touched-up photograph. Visitors were expected and encouraged. Orange, purple, and green banners waved in the still summer air as we clamored onto the wooden bridge that led into the resort. Excitement oozed near the covered tram that pulled up willing passengers to the top of the mountain. Their faces told me that there were few skiers in the group.

Delicate sounds nudged me as I sauntered by an open-air shop. Wind chimes of all sizes and shapes made from metal, shells, rocks, and just about everything teetered from metallic tree limbs. Huge blue chunks of sparkling agate dangled from toughened strings that clang harmoniously together. Captured by their song, I purchased two stone wind chimes. It would be a perfect gift for anyone. In the next shop, painted wooden and metal bird houses hung on simulated tree branches. Nature products were everywhere. But I longed for the real thing.

The winding stream cast its spell. Its source baffled me. Walking along its banks, I was mesmerized by the large smooth stones that crisscrossed the stream. The child in me jumped out leaping on one slippery rock after the other. Before I knew it, each of my legs landed on separate rocks, and I tumbled in the numbing cold water up to my knees. Snickering laughter echoed down the stream. Birds didn't laugh, and I was by myself. Then looking upward, I saw them—three curious boys perched on an extended tree limb with big eyes and grinning mouths. I was their afternoon entertainment. In or out of trees, boys were boys. Relieved that the laughter belonged to someone, I ignored them.

"Hey are you okay?" one of the boys bellowed. "This is our lookout station." Pointing the youngest boy giggled. "We live over there."

Not far from the stream, a fancy chalet with broad pine beams tucked itself into the woods. These kids had no idea how fortunate they were or maybe they did. My seventh graders, disadvantaged students would be thrilled just to look at this stream, let alone live on it. Did anyone ever appreciate what they had? The boys' cries faded as I quickly continued down the stream, ever aware of my footing. The sun soaked through my numbness. Refreshed, I only had soggy sneakers and not soggy clothes. When I just about gave up my quest for the stream's source, illuminated water splashed and danced in front of me.

It was a waterfall. The kind in stories. A scent of fresh rain permeated my senses. I forgot how pure water could be since we weren't supposed to drink unfiltered water back home. A distinct rushing sound rumbled underneath the ground as part of the waterfall vanished right before me. Spying an unannounced opening behind the tumbling water, I carefully walked into the misty spray. The opening was just wide enough for one person to pass through. I half expected nymphs to invite me in. I guess I've read too many children's books. Listening behind a waterfall sounds very different than listening in front of one.

It was very faint but then grew louder. A little girl's voice crying. And there sitting on a rock was a child covered with dirt and ripped jeans. The very last thing I expected to see.

"I lost my brothers. We were playing a game. They just left me here." Hysterical, the young child could hardly talk. I guess I was supposed to be here.

"Look I am a teacher and will help you like your teacher would at school okay? Let's kind of play our own game and see how long it takes us to find your brothers." That did it the crying stopped. She hobbled up to me and put her hand in mine. Whatever happens to all of that trust?

I just had a hunch where her brothers were. Retracing my steps, I was confronted with her hysterical mom. It was genetic. The little girl clung to her mother for dear life. The mother didn't want any explanation, evidently she knew her sons very well. Thank you wasn't necessary. Hopefully, anyone would have done the very same thing. It only confirmed my opinion that very young kids needed to be on a long leash no matter how silly it might look. Now I was more aware of just what you might find in the woods.

Time called me back. Before my water adventure, a blue-and-white handwoven Norwegian ski sweater dangled gracefully in a shop window, grabbing my attention. That very shop was only a block away. It wasn't that I needed the sweater, or would even wear it in Texas, well maybe once or twice, but it was so beautifully Nordic. To have a warm reminder of Vail would be memorable, and maybe someday I would go skiing again. It reminded me of my dad's well-worn, thread-bare Vermont ski sweater that he refused to give up. Indulging, I bought it. I would probably never wear it, but at least I could look at it. Half of my clothes fell into that category.

When everyone responded to their announced name, Mr. Hudson breathed easier. All seats were filled, and no one had been maimed getting on and off the mountain's tram. As the bus started down the steep incline, there were no sounds of grunting or groaning. Robert Frost's poetic words came to mind. Miles to go before I sleep.

There were many miles to go before we reached Arches National Park in Moab, Utah since we were presently in Vail, Colorado. The states that we visited shared hot humid weather and mountainous terrain.

Excited, Mr. Moles, a weekend archeologist, passed around some photographs of the magnificent arches that he acquired from a friend who just returned from this very bus trip.

"This is one of the main reasons that I chose this trip to see nature's naturally carved arches by wind and random erosion." Mr. Moles couldn't wait to share his knowledge. "How the arches actually formed can be attributed to the huge underlying salt bed that sits underneath the park. Millions of years ago, the ocean flooded the area and then somehow it evaporated. Layers of sandstone were deposited on one another, and the salt bed below liquefied and pushed up, creating salt domes. As millions of years passed, water crept into the crevices, ice formed and expanded, and the pressure changed the rocks. Arches appeared. As you can see in the pictures, the arches' sandstone is salmon or buff colored."

"When I researched the park, I found out that since 1970, more than forty arches out of 2,000 have collapsed. There is no time like the present to see what remains of the 119 square miles of the park."

Looking at the names under the photographs, I could see how the arches' identifying features matched their spirited names: Dark Angel, Balanced Rock, Devil's Garden, and the Three Gossips. Facts from the other parks swept through my mind.

"Was this one of President Roosevelt's protected parks like many of the others?" I asked a surprised Mr. Moles.

"Yes, it was. And in 1969, President Johnson enlarged the park, but President Nixon reduced its size two years later changing it to a national park."

Leon's words repeated themselves. "How could rocks be so fascinating?" These were, and I couldn't wait to see them. When returning, maybe weekend archeology would be a possibility.

"The arches must entice rock climbers." Envisioning swinging dare devils joined together with a single rope.

Mr. Moles pointed out. "It is prohibited on the actual arches but hiking, camping, and biking are allowed elsewhere in the park. When Edward Abbey published his book *Desert Solitaire*, he used his journals as a park ranger. Everyone wanted to see the prickly pear cactus, evening primrose, yucca plants, toads, lizards, big horn sheep, mountain lions, falcons, and other creatures."

A park ranger, an author, a book. Intrigued, I wanted to experience the raw beauty for myself. Pleased, Mr. Moles noticed my interest and questions. His wife also noticed and wasn't pleased.

"That's the one that has caused all of the disruption on this bus. The couple from Australia told me that Sara always cries for her husband."

"Wouldn't you if I were not able to be with you on this trip?" Mrs. Moles clammed up like a tangled up clam. Nothing else came out of her mouth. She couldn't keep quiet for long. Public opinion swayed Mrs. Moles, but she finally decided to find out for herself.

"Sara, I heard that you were a school teacher. What grade do you teach?"

I really didn't want to talk to Mrs. Moles but it was unavoidable. Every instinct in me said no, but my mouth answered. Next to his wife sat Mr. Moles. What possibly could be misconstrued? Everything.

"Seventh grade, low income, disadvantaged students." The more I talked, the more interested Mrs. Moles appeared. My real feelings about learning leaked out.

"I think young boys and girls...well all boys and girls should go to separate schools. They concentrate better, and the girls don't have to worry about how they look and what they say, alienating themselves from one another." Frustrated, Mrs. Moles became a puffed-up blowfish.

"I have never heard such nonsense in all my life. How unnatural, how elitist. Boys and girls belong together. They have to learn how to get along with one another. I always appreciated the boys in my classes. They didn't affect me one way or the other." Mr. Moles couldn't help but hear the conversation as did others and wanted to disarm his indignant wife.

"What about me, didn't I affect you?"

"That was entirely different."

"There is probably more than one way to look at this issue." Mr. James offered. "I, for one, support segregated classes. As a professor at the university level I think, there are probably too many female distractions in our classrooms in the mini auditoriums where we teach our classes. Actually our dropout rate is rather high and consists of many young, undisciplined female students."

Mr. James didn't want to listen to Mrs. Mole's caustic remarks. He wasn't going to put up with an inexperienced educator. Grateful, I jumped out when Mr. James jumped in. Fifty was the age limit. Older minds tightened with crippling steel clamps. Within seconds, my mind was wrapped around the openness of Mozart and the arches' beauty. Mrs. Moles' comments were faint puffs of smoke that didn't cling to me.

Utah. Percy couldn't wait. The more miles between South Dakota and the moving bus the better. Colorado was still too close. Percy was grateful for my silence. No one had any inkling about her fascination with Crazy Horse. Everyone just assumed that Percy blacked out, injuring herself slightly when she fell. Support and helpful advice about dizzy spells was offered. I never pried, never asked. Percy never offered. A silent guard stood erectly between us.

Meg watched Percy. She wished she knew why Percy fainted and why I was always in the middle of everything that happened to anyone on this bus. Ever since the accident, Martha confidently confided in Meg that Percy was bewitched. Over and over like a worn out mantra, Martha insisted that she had completely changed. Refusing to listen, Meg thought that it was sheer nonsense and utterly ridiculous.

Martha refocused on Percy's odd behavior. Being an atheist she was secretly delighted when Christians toppled. A bewitched Christian, Martha couldn't wait to spread it around the bus.

A few bored summers ago without telling her husband, Martha had dabbled in terra cards thinking there was something to it. Percy exhibited some of the black flags. Disorientated, and quiet, Sara didn't even seem to want to talk with Percy.

Martha's slurping reminded thirsty Percy of a frothy ice cream shake. Within a minute, Martha casually offered Percy some of her slushy, icy drink pouring it into a paper cup. Percy couldn't believe her eyes.

"Does your head still ache?" Martha pointedly asked, observing Percy's every reaction, waiting for her to cringe. Percy just smiled.

"My headaches are gone, but I was really thirsty. You must be a mind reader." Martha was taken back. Percy was one step ahead of her.

"It must have been a terrible fall. Without thinking, someone must have forgotten and left an empty water bottle behind that you tripped over. Or maybe there was an enlarged tree root that caught your toe and caused you to fall."

"I don't recall any bottles or any tree roots. Losing your balance, I guess happens at one time or another to all of us."

"It has never happened to me." Agitated, Martha was getting nowhere quickly. Percy wasn't going to open up to her. There didn't seem to be anything to open up. Determined, Martha tried another tact. "Sometimes when people are unconscious, certain things remain in their mind."

"You know you are right. I do remember something. Blueberries, the scent of blueberries."

"You probably landed in a patch." Meg watched Martha's drilling techniques fail. Evidently, the only witch on the bus might have been Martha herself.

Not even waiting for his wife, an eager Mr. Moles was the first off the bus. Grinning, I watched as the young boy in Mr. Moles emerged. Mr. Hito, and Joel the other avid photographers in the group had some competition. From a distance, I followed Mr. Moles knowing he would be an inquisitive scout.

Fanning out, the arches' muted colors softened into mustard and tangerine tones under the lowering sun. There were only a few hours of light remaining. The photographs didn't fully reveal the bending in the arches. In the Martian landscape, the arches' openings were enormous. And looked as if Giants had walked through the sandstones leaving their graphic imprints.

Some of the women, who were more interested in talking than looking, lingered towards the back. Hikers sprung ahead like released rubber bands. Further up ahead, some of the adventurers started climbing up one of the larger arches. The group was unescorted. Mr. Hudson was nowhere in sight. Three climbers made it up to the top of the arch when a horse-saddled ranger appeared on the horizon. Evidently, these three had not heeded Mr. Moles' instructions or the regulations—don't climb the arches.

Joking freely and completely unaware of their trespassing, the three offenders commended themselves on their achievement when an irate ranger abruptly dismounted ordering them to come down. Looking like three sheepish school boys, the violators slowly descended as the meticulous ranger copied down their personal information. Mr. Hudson appeared when he was needed. His professional eyes latched on to the annoyed ranger.

"I am the tour director for this group. It appears that not everyone remembered the stipulations regarding climbing." The uniformed ranger wasn't amused.

"There is a hefty fine for trespassing on the arches. It needs to be paid before you depart from the park."

The ranger handed an embarrassed, red faced Mr. Hudson the designated fine. It would be all over the park within minutes. Mr. Hudson's competent reputation was in jeopardy. Any complaints filed against a tour director would be cancerous growth that left nothing behind. No one would hire you if you couldn't control your group's behavior.

Hesitating, the three climbers approached Mr. Hudson. Letting out a huge sigh of relief, Mr. Hudson didn't recognize any of them. They were not part of his group.

"Where is your group?"

"We don't have a group. We are on our own."

"Didn't you even get a brochure about the park? This is a national park, and the arches are protected. You can't climb on the arches. It is against the regulations."

"We don't follow regulations."

"You will after reading this. It is $100.00 fine for each of you. If you don't pay it, you will be arrested. Enjoy the rest of your time here at the park." With that said, Mr. Hudson gladly handed over the fine to the men and walked away.

Audience or no audience, the incident just reinforced how important it was that the parks' regulations were enforced. No longer following one another, we all scattered like pent-up children on a playground.

I was comfortably lost in the arches when an excited high-pitched voice called out. "I found it, I really found it."

The cry belonged to Mr. Moles. I couldn't see him, but I followed his faint echo that whispered among the arches. Imagining all sorts of things, I only hoped that it wasn't anything mummified. Covered with dirt, Mr. Moles was on his hands and knees digging furiously in the reddened earth. Beside him was a big chunk of limestone that he had unearthed.

"Sara, look closely at the layers of sediment. Do you see them, the crustaceans?"

I remembered that Mr. Moles had mentioned that the sea covered this area millions of years ago. Distinctly preserved, the fossils looked as though they might just wiggle out of the rock. This find could only excite an archeologist.

"Sara, do you want to help me dig?" I didn't. Just as Mr. Moles asked, a stylish Mrs. Moles stepped into view fully protected from the sun with a broad rimmed hat, long, loose sleeves, and mid-calf pants.

"That won't be necessary. I will help you, dear." Relieved, I never thought that hearing Mrs. Moles' voice could be so pleasant. It was difficult imagining her delicate hands digging in Martian dirt. Pleased with his wife's support, Mr. Moles carefully instructed her how to separate crumbling layers of sandstone for fossils. Released from digging even before I started, I quickly exited. All of Mrs. Moles' energy needed to be directed towards the earth, not me.

After a while, many of the windswept arches looked familiar. Differing only in size and shape, they had similar colors and openings. The heat of the day locked onto me, and I felt almost as tired as the million year old arches. Others also wilted since there wasn't a shady tree in sight. The craving for Martian sandstone faded. With his blistered reddened hands and fossil encrusted rocks, even Mr. Moles was ready to go. No one wanted to bother Mr. Hudson by suggesting that we leave. No one had to; the roundup commenced.

I never thought that I would be anxious to get back on any bus. Every tired muscle in my body felt abused. It was the nearing end of the second week, and I still lacked endurance. My hiking days were quickly coming to an end.

"Look at her. She can't take it. She belongs in a rest home."

The male voice whispered just loud enough for me to hear. The voice's tone was different from the others. Maybe it was heat stroke. Shutting it out, I couldn't get my headphones on fast enough.

There was just enough energy in me to call Leon. Snuggled in a rustic-looking bed with pine knotted boughs I was comforted by Leon's voice.

"You called. Sara, you sound so far away, so tired. What is wrong, are you sick?" Leon expected me to be filled with my usual unraveling energy. There was no rippling effect of any kind on the other end of the line.

"Leon, I am just so worn out. By now, I just assumed that I would be in better shape."

"Guess what? Tomorrow we are crossing the state line and heading back towards southern Colorado to Mesa Verde National Park where the Anasazi Indians built their dwellings in the cliffs."

"What state are you in now?"

"Utah. Leon, I just wanted to call and tell you that your voice was the only one I wanted to hear."

"Sara, I know that this trip has been difficult for you but remember it was your choice."

I knew only too well what my husband said was true. Little did I know that my real testing hadn't even started.

THE CLIFF DWELLINGS

AS I PEERED DOWNWARD, THE openings in the cliffs were masked. Still too far away to see the details, I headed downward toward the raging river that crisscrossed the settlement. There was something about the force of the water that commanded my attention. In front of me, numerous waterfalls cascaded down upon one another as others photographed the mist. You were only permitted to get so close. It was too close. Unattended, a little foot got too near to the saturated railing, lost its balance and slipped. One minute the little boy was there and the next minute he wasn't. Everything in me stopped. Now I fully understood why nothing prevented me from going on this trip.

As if rehearsed, I quickly lowered myself off the ramp, hung over the edge and dropped. Cold, icy water bit into my skin. Numbness invaded me as I heard a muffled whimpering cry that echoed fear. Near the river's edge, the distraught little boy had somehow tangled himself up in brushwood, which blocked him from the river's grasp. Washing up towards the opposite side, I battled the current trying to get to him. Relentlessly, the determined water pushed me back harder and harder. It was useless. The child couldn't be reached.

My combat with the current ended while the shallow moving water pulled me downstream. The thought of more waterfalls tugged at me. Slowing down, my numbed arms and legs were not moving as quickly. The river knew. Somehow I had to get out of it. Ahead of me, a stretched-out, sturdy log protruded over the bank. Grabbing for the weathered log, I pulled my exhausted body on top of it and collapsed. In a lifeless stupor, my mind raced. A child deserved a chance to grow up. A young life couldn't be taken away so randomly.

In the distance, I heard my name shouted over and over again and slowly opened my eyes. The voices might not be real. But the hollering continued, getting closer.

Meanwhile an astonished Mr. Hudson couldn't believe his ears when a usually calm, level-headed Dr. James bounded up the path towards him yelling frantically woman over railing. It made no sense.

"Someone pushed Sara into the rapids, into the river. She has disappeared from sight."

"Dr. James, get a hold of yourself." Mr. Hudson felt ridiculous after he said it. After all, who was he to talk that way to a learned professor. "Did you actually see someone push Sara in?"

"Well no. But it looked like Sara struggled against the current, trying to get out." Whoever it was needs help quickly, or you may have a body on your hands."

Mr. Hudson's insides turned to mush. A body? Someone in this chilly river? Anybody but Sara. It couldn't be Sara. What if it were Sara? Her husband would put a contract out on him immediately making sure that he never worked or even breathed again. His mind quickly resurfaced as panicked hikers were running all over the place.

Toppling into Mr. Hudson, Meg cried out. "There was a little boy who tripped past the railing and fell over. Someone jumped in to save the boy." Mr. Hudson didn't need to hear another word. It was Sara. He had to find her alive.

No one had waited for Mr. Hudson. Hearing the boy's moans, a few men sprung down the embankment pulling a quivering little boy out of clinging brushwood. At her wits' end, his mother couldn't get him in her arms quickly enough.

My arms were wrapped around a log. The more I listened, the more familiar the voices seemed.

"There she is. Over there, it's Sara on top of that decayed log."

Wading into the river ahead of the others, Percy couldn't get to me fast enough. Indebted, Percy now had a chance to repay my kindness.

"Sara, everyone is searching for you. Are you hurt? Here, put this blanket around you. Dry clothes are on their way."

Massaging my arms and legs, Percy knew that my circulation needed to be jump started like a frozen car's engine. Tinted faded blue lips and white shriveled fingers were the river's frostbite.

Everyone felt that determined Percy would not come out of the woods empty handed. A prepared coffee drinker had even handed Percy a hot thermos of coffee...

"Sara, drink this."

The strong taste and pungent aroma of black coffee brought me back. "There was a little boy."

"He is safe."

"How in the world did you find me?"

"Because I needed to. I didn't want Crazy Horse to get his hands on you."

I really didn't know if Percy were joking or not, I didn't care. Just feeling warmth, I realized that the river might have beaten me. "Percy, thank you. Thank you for everything."

"No, I should be the one thanking you." Momentarily, Percy looked away. Our arms wrapped around one another's shoulders. Our spontaneous laughter rippled down the river.

"What are you girls laughing about?" asked a dumbfounded Mr. Moles who followed closely in Percy's footsteps. "Sara, you are so lucky. There are more waterfalls further downstream. You spotted that log just in the nick of time." In spite of his wife's misgivings, Mr. Moles was extremely fond of Sara. Heaving a huge sigh of relief, Mr. Moles also laughed in spite of himself. Pushing through the brush, concerned searchers found three drenched laughing river rats. Their laughter was contagious.

"Let me through, let me through," shouted a frenzied Mr. Hudson. "Is it Sara? Is she okay?" Confused Mr. Hudson didn't appreciate the laughter. It only upset him all the more.

"I am okay, Mr. Hudson. Just took an unexpected swim." Tears of bottled-up joy slowly spilled down Mr. Hudson's face as he realized that his own life had also been spared. With a grateful heart, Mr. Hudson laughed heaving like a madman.

After the rescued excitement had quieted down, a warmed up entourage headed for the cliff's ancient dwellings. Nearing the bottom of the scaling rocks, Percy looked up feeling a strong Indian attraction. Immediately, she stopped it. Mesmerized, I focused on the artisan handiwork peering at the primitive carved out niches. And to think it was all done without sandblasters.

In addition to being avid farmers, Mr. Hudson explained that the Pueblo Indians were also creative builders using mud, sandstone, and adobe to construct their dwellings.

"As you can see, the cliff dwellings were built out of caves and under overhanging rocks. From ad 550 to ad 1300, the Pueblo Indians also known as the Anasazi lived here in this area." Lifting the veil of time, the families weaved their famous baskets and stained their much sought after pottery. "As with other historical sites, the Pueblos' artifacts were in high demand and much of the architecture was pilfered and damaged. Sadly it is often still the case today." Mankind was very greedy destroying nearly everything that they set foot on. "Spanish explorers founded the area and were followed by ranchers. Mineralogists and photographers damaged the original dwellings. One in particular removed countless artifacts and tried to sell them in Finland and Switzerland. Even that faraway, he was hunted down and almost killed. In 1906, Teddy Roosevelt protected Mesa Verde from further vandalism by making it into a national park." Thankful for the president's actions, I inhaled the dwelling's beauty knowing that it could have been easily trampled into oblivion.

The flanked entourage divided up, leaving Percy, Meg, and me trailing behind. Curious, Meg was determined to find out what really happened in that river. She just couldn't believe that anyone jumped into an icy death sentence to save a boy. Meg doubted whether there even was a boy. The whole thing was probably made up. Attention, it all centered around attention. Everyone catered to Sara, worrying about her, befriending her. Now, Percy and Sara were inseparable.

Negative energy flooded me even before I saw Meg. Lingering in one of the tiny makeshift rooms, I squeezed through an opening just large enough to get through to the next room. Dieting wasn't necessary back then. Halfway up the mud walls were windows that didn't even come up to my shoulders. The Indians dwarfed in stature compared to today's giants. Meg's voice didn't.

"Hey, I just couldn't believe what I heard. Come on, Sara, did a boy really fall into the river? I mean did you really see someone? Maybe you just thought you saw someone." That did it. I didn't like Meg's tone or her innuendos.

"No, I jumped in because I was so hot. Is that what you want to hear?" There were only three days left. I forgot the sound of harassment. Remembering, I didn't like what I heard. I no longer cared. Once the trip was over, I was extremely certain that I would never see any of these people again.

Meg was taken back. She had expected the sweet unassuming Sara. That Sara was gone; the river had washed her away. "It just all seems so unbelievable. It just always seems to happen around you."

Over hearing the conversation, Percy noticed Sara and Meg crouched in the same dwelling, in the same room. Percy didn't like Meg or her sidekick Martha who was her best buddy.

"Sara, hurry up. Can you take my picture from here?" It was Percy, and I couldn't wait to focus the camera's lenses.

"Oh, is that your bodyguard?" Meg smiled, baiting me. "We wouldn't want to disappoint her, would we?" Everything in me wanted to punch Meg. The thought sickened me, but I almost did it. If twelve-year-old girls at school did it...that stopped me, I wasn't twelve, and this wasn't about any boy. In my mind, I punched her and turned away.

Percy also wanted to take some pictures of me from within one of the makeshift dwellings. Leon would be surprised how well crafted the cave homes were. After a few camera clicks, we ambled up the trail. That's when I heard it. Pained voices drifted down from the cliff dwellings. Someone was hurt. Someone needed help. Percy didn't even flinch. Behind us, Meg slowly plodded along not taking her eyes off the dirt trail.

Panic stopped me. I had to try. Then I remembered that Indians didn't like to be photographed believing it took part of their souls. Could it have been the pictures? It didn't make any sense. Nothing that happened to me today made any sense. Did our pictures capture something that was forbidden? Why couldn't Percy hear the voices?

Blocking the sounds, I talked over them. Percy couldn't understand why I kept talking louder and louder. Wailing eerily, one voice ascended above the others.

"You will not get away from us. Sacred ground has been violated." After that wonderful, harassing thought, the sounds abruptly faded and left. Percy took one long look at my face and hesitated.

"Sara, do you want to rest?" Rest—that was the last thing on my mind. I couldn't get away from the cliff dwellings fast enough.

"Percy, have you heard anything around us like maybe birds or rumblings or even conversation?"

"The only thing I may have heard was behind us, Meg muttering about something, about the river. That was all. Sara, did you hear them? I mean do you think you heard someone?"

"There were voices, like the ones I heard when we rafted on the river. But these were closer more distinct. They were angry, and they were Indian."

Percy palled. It was all her fault. Sara had rescued her from Crazy Horse, and now they were after her. Glancing at Percy, Sara realized she said way too much without thinking. Sullen, Percy looked as if she were marooned on a violated, pirate-kidnapped cruise ship. Sara quickly backtracked.

"It was probably nothing. Today's events were just...just so surreal. Percy, do you remember reading in your book about how the Indians never wanted their pictures taken even today because they believe it takes away a portion of their souls? That thought just wouldn't leave me alone. My unexpected river ride just got the best of me." Gradually, color returned to Percy's drained face. We both walked faster.

Glancing back at Meg, I knew she no longer bothered me. Any future conversation with her was insignificant. On the other hand, Percy nagged at me. Since her traumatized fall, she needed reassurance and sound reasoning. My vivid imagination was overruled. Regardless of what happened during the next three days, Percy and I were going to enjoy the rest of this trip. Tomorrow's visit to Kayenta, the Indian Reservation, would undo my determined words.

Today rattled me. The little boy, the river, the rescue, the Indian entourage, it was front-page material. Most of it was just unbelievable.

Leon would never believe it. Then and there, I decided that I wouldn't tell him. If I did, Mr. Hudson would be a tour-less guide and someone would have to explain why. I didn't want to be that someone. What happened on this river would remain here until I got home. Up ahead were figures and suddenly I heard a little voice.

"Mommy, mommy that is the lady, the water warrior who tried to save me." Tugging at my hand, Berto reached into his parched pocket and carefully pulled out a delicate wilted purple wildflower.

"I wanted you to have this. It's beautiful and reminded me of you. I will never forget what you did for me. Thank you for giving me back to my mommy."

Being a teacher, I sometimes got little gifts from my students, but nothing like this. My words weren't ready. Seeing Berto's hand clutched to his mothers said it all. Promising never to lose it, I placed the little wilted purple flower into my parched pocket.

THE INDIAN
RESERVATION

TODAY WAS A BRAND NEW day. On a whim, I decided to do something that I haven't done since I was sixteen, horseback riding. At the Kayenta Indian Reservation, a group of riders signed up for the excursion, and one horse needed a rider. Filling the empty saddle, I was neck and neck with the snorting independent mare. It opened up bottled-up horseback riding camp memories.

It was summer. I was sixteen, on the back of a chestnut-brown mare horse who wanted absolutely nothing to do with me. With a full brisk mane and stubborn eyes, my hungry horse was determined to get rid of me. Following behind the other trail-trained horses, my horse suddenly broke line, galloped madly into the woods, dodging birch limbs and brush trying in vain to scrape me off his back. Being unsuccessful, he tried another tactic. Slowing down, my spirited horse came to a complete halt, as I tumbled over his head landing in the middle of the field. Certain that I was crippled for life, I carefully examined my arms and legs. Surprisingly, they moved.

Very pleased with himself, the crafty horse then returned inspecting the damage. Evidently, he didn't like what he saw and charged me.

"Get up, get up!" My horseback-riding instructor demanded that I move. I did. But much to my tear drenched horror, I was instructed to get right back on that very horse. The riding teacher was insane. Her insistence provoked me and the horse. No sooner had I settled back into the twisted saddle and regained a bit of my self-confidence, the horse reared its head, kneeled, and rolled. Somehow, my right leg was wedged in the saddle, and I couldn't free it. Again all I heard was "Get up, get up!" That did it. Extremely annoyed, I almost yanked my leg off freeing myself just before the horse collapsed on top of me. I refused to get back on that horse. I haven't been on one since.

The excited riders drowned out the memories. Hoping the horses were well fed, I peered into a pair of glazed beautiful brown eyes belonging to a chestnut mare. She whinnied. There was an instant understanding between us. She didn't mind me on her back. The dusty trail etched its way through the stark reservation. There was nothing to see except flat, dry land that stretched out for miles and miles. I could understand why the Indians hated it. Up ahead of us, our Indian guide was in his native dress, and I could almost picture the way it was. Suddenly pouncing on us like prey, a band of shrieking cowboys riding bareback blocked the trail. Stampeding, the horses turned in all directions. Unabashed, my confident horse seemed to know just what to do and galloped steadily towards a hidden ravine further up ahead.

At least they weren't Indians. It kept running through my mind. I didn't want to meet Crazy Horse or any other irate Anasazi or Navajo Indian alone on a horse on this reservation. Percy's demise still clung to me.

In the distance were scattered dusty reddened monoliths. I made myself remember what I read. Back in the 1800s, when this land was a trading post, some of the monoliths were named after miners who prospected for silver. Before them, Spanish and Mexican explorers scouted the area but were confronted with Navajo Indian raids. The only raids now were against unsuspecting tourists. This reservation was enlarged and protected by President Chester Arthur. Where was all of this presidential protection when we needed it?

Quickly approaching the spiraling monoliths, ancient survivors of some 270 million years, I saw the radiant reddish iron oxide and pure black streaks of manganese oxide. Their layers of sandstone, siltstone, and shale were lifted up then folded by volcanic eruptions and eroded by the weather. Some of the dikes that survived were 1,500 feet tall. One was before me.

The monoliths stared in some of the famous Western movies that were filmed here thirty years ago. John Wayne acted in those movies. Could this possibly be a movie set? The cowboys on those horses didn't even slightly resemble the famous actor. No one would have watched this movie.

I couldn't hear a sound from the other horses or the other riders. The only audible sound was the breathing of my tired horse as his hoofs dug into the dirt. The quiet was broken by the baying of sheep. A lone Indian herded a flock of sheep trailed by a mangy sheep dog. The old weathered Indian didn't seem to notice me or if he did he didn't care. Thousands of tourists visited this reservation. But with blond hair flying like a tangled flag, alone, on a horse, in the middle of a ravine? The old Indian couldn't have missed me. Maybe he couldn't see me.

Lining the ravine were jutting rocks etched with figures and animals. These had to be the petroglyphs, which revealed the Indian's story, their ancient ways, and customs. I wondered if any of these rocks were also the ones that had supernatural powers according to the Indian lore. Totem Pole Rock was a skinny spiraling rock that was thought to be a God held up by lightning. It would have been so interesting to have the rocks identified by the Indian guide. Right now that was surreal. I had no idea where the Indian guide was or if there even was one. And I paid for this?

Slowing down, my horse walked carefully across the slanted ravine. Ahead in the loosened rocks was a bearded cowboy twirling a lasso above his head. Cringing, I didn't know what to do. My horse knew exactly what to do and quickly changed directions charging back up the ravine. Digging my heels into his sides, I stayed fastened to his sloping back. The incessant swishing rope didn't stop until it hit its target, my horse's vulnerable neck. It might as well have been mine. My anger shouted.

"Get you slimy hands off my horse. What kind of a lame cowboy are you? Cordoning off a lone woman on a horse. You need to take more lessons."

"It wasn't supposed to be like this. You were supposed to stay with the rest of the riders. This horse never does."

"It is over. If you don't get that rope off my horse, I will sue you for anything and everything that you have."

"I am a cowboy. I don't have anything. You will follow me. The others have already been rounded up."

"You will never round me up." My horse's headlock had loosened. I barely pulled the rope off when my angry horse reared toppling the astonished cowboy off his own surprised horse. Winnowing in pride, my horse nudged my leg with his cheek, and turned galloping across the open land in front of him.

An intercom blasted through the air as though commanding a fall football team. "You need to stop your horse. We are running out of time." Running out of time? As if on cue, my horse recognized the familiar projected voice and stopped. Over to one side, the other riders were bunched together contentedly, munching on watermelon and feeding it to their horses.

"Didn't anyone tell you that this is a reenactment trail ride? The cowboys were positioned on the trails on purpose. It was supposed to add novelty to the ride."

"No, no one bothered to tell me. It was not at all novel. In fact, you are extremely lucky that I didn't fall off this horse during his frantic galloping."

"Your horse does tend to get carried away but is well-trained and knew just what to do. He takes his favorites to the ravine." An exhausted voice interrupted us.

"You can get yourself a new cowboy. I quit. That crazy horse nearly killed me with that crazy lady on its back. Her horse reared in my face. Retaliating, my own horse then threw me head first in the dirt. I think I broke my arm."

Was that all part of the reenactment as well? Disgusted, I didn't listen to the rest of it as my crazy horse and I joined the other riders more than ready for our own piece of watermelon. Regaining my composure, I told everyone what happened. Disbelief then cheers erupted when the other participants realized that I just didn't know.

Once again, we clamored into our saddles, ready for the remainder of the trail. Without harassing cowboys, it was uneventful. With both of my feet firmly on the ground, I knew that this horse would join my other bottled-up horseback riding memories. I doubted if I would ever want to get back into another saddle on another horse on another trail.

On an open air bus, we explored the rest of the reservation. Mr. Hudson didn't let me out of his sight. Sitting a seat away from me, he wanted to reassure himself that I wasn't going to disappear. Tired, I tried listening to what Enlightened Eyes, the Indian lady tour guide shared about her people and their struggles. I couldn't help but notice her totem, a tiny tattoo, on her left hand. What did it mean? She caught me starring and thrust her hand into her pocket. Her prying brown eyes stared back at me, examining my soul. Everything in me wanted to apologize. I knew better than to stare. My rudeness was trampled on. I was an ugly white woman with no manners. My stomach tightened. I felt something linger over me, waiting. I had to get off this bus. Abruptly, her speech ended. Dollar bills were randomly stuffed into her anticipating tip bucket. Enlightened Eyes nodded gratefully. Her grateful eyes ignored me completely.

Near the parking lot, handmade Indian wares were displayed proudly on makeshift tables. When each handicraft was examined closely, hopeful eyes lit up one by one. Nature symbols were crafted into almost every piece. Bags weren't needed. Almost everyone wore what they bought. Sprinkled in turquoise, each one of us took a tiny bit of the reservation with us as we left.

Unwrapping my purchase, I wondered if Leon would like the turquoise inlaid money clip. I couldn't wait to call him with clues about his gift. The phone just rang. No one answered. Did I dial the right number? I tried again. My stomach tightened. Leon always answered. Like a gusty wind, uneasiness swept through me.

"He doesn't really care. He isn't there. He didn't wait." I heard the words repeat themselves. The words weren't mine. I would never even think that. Was this part of a plan? Did I eat anything on the reservation? I hadn't eaten all day. My water bottle never left the bus. Did I inhale something? No strange smells were on the bus. Smoking anything was prohibited.

The totem on the Indian guide's hand twisted around my mind. Her piercing brown eyes demanded something. Why didn't I apologize? Why didn't I take the time?

Very alone, it was my turn to feel vulnerable. I realized what Leon felt when I didn't call. Was Leon hurt? Did he fall? Was he ill? Where was he?

Questions gnawed at me. Troubled sleep embraced me. Answers would have to wait until tomorrow.

THE GRAND CANYON

MISSING A FEW HOURS OF sleep, I was thankful for the monotonous bus ride. With big bags under my eyes, I camouflaged my circles with my sunglasses. I didn't want Mr. Hudson or anyone else prying. There was only one reason. It would remain unknown.

When a trip nears the end, you sense it. Sometimes the best was saved for last. Many on this trip were on this bus because of today, wanting to see the grandeur of the Grand Canyon. Talk about ancient. Millions of years were nothing compared to this canyon. It was billions of years old. In all of that time, the Colorado River never gave up eroding the land winding the canyon this way and that.

Someone once told me if I ever had the chance to see the Grand Canyon not to miss the river rafting. It was scheduled for tomorrow. Today we would have time to explore around the rim and venture down any trails that lead into the canyon. Something so beautiful was also deadly. Reenactments on television depicting parched, lost, defeated hikers sprawled alone prepared to die on deserted trails jumped into my mind.

Posted advisories were everywhere and expected to be followed. In this canyon, water was life. Bottled water was a necessity. Hiking down into the canyon alone without a trail guide was done at your own risk. The park was not responsible for losses. I shuddered at the thought. Water bottles were crammed into knapsacks and pockets as tightly laced up sneakers and aimed cameras were ready to document the canyon's beauty.

The immensity of the canyon swallowed me up. Layers of cliffs with reddened rocks and determined trees spiraled downward towards the winding Colorado River that someone sketched in. Many tour groups were bunched together. I became one with the crowd.

The canyon's beauty harassed me, commanding my complete undivided attention. The rim's path was about ten feet away from the edge, still too close for those who didn't realize that they were claustrophobic. Concentrating on my pace, I wanted to get away from the others. The artist in me wanted a private showing.

The rim's path stretched for miles along side the horizon. I decided to allot two hours for exploring and two hours for returning. One hour would be set aside for everything else, the gift shop, bookstore, photographs, and relaxation. The long-lined ice cream shop would be my last stop.

Pine trees insisted on growing out of or between rocks. They were not overtaken or denied by the intense heat, shifting rocks, or violent winds. As I passed camera buffs, I couldn't believe how close to the edge the posers poised.

He was also very close to the edge. I couldn't help but overhear the dare. His two friends dared him to jump over a small opening between two rocks on the rim's edge. It was death's trigger. Everything in me stopped. I didn't intervene. He was directly in front of me. If he slipped or misjudged the distance, the canyon's arms would hold him forever. He jumped, laughing, landing safely on the second rock.

Why taunt life? Glimpses of terminally ill children filled my eyes. They were not given a choice to breathe on their own, to heal on their own, or to walk on their own without dragging along attached critical life supporting tubes. Why didn't that fool realize how fortunate he was? Not telling him, I fought myself. There wasn't a lot of arguing room on the trail. Passing him, I turned my disgusted face the other way, quickening my pace.

The urge to peer down into the canyon's soul grew stronger and stronger. Closer and closer I crept to the edge.

Words echoed from out of the belly of the canyon. "There she is walking as if she owned the entire trail, not saying a word to anyone. Why should we even bother? It won't affect her at all."

The conversation could have been from anyone about anyone. I only hoped it wasn't coming from the three daredevils that I just passed. But it was a woman's voice, an elderly voice, a tired voice.

"It wouldn't take much. She is already hurrying."

I didn't listen. Maybe it was an annoyed someone from the crowd that I had bumped into or brushed by accident. There were just so many people everywhere.

Bit by bit, the canyon's beauty waned. Fatigue took over.

Afternoon shadows fell around me, outlining a familiar figure on the path. It was Enlightened Eye's totem having the same shape, the same wings, and the same talons. Shrieking with its mouth and lifting its wings, the eagle floated effortlessly down into the canyon's depths. Mesmerized, I almost lost my balance and grabbed onto a look-out's railing with my left hand. This was Indian territory. I felt it. There were no ancestral ruins here to violate. But what lay beneath us in the canyon's abyss? Part of me wanted to know. The other part didn't.

I failed to see her. She crept closer to me, startling me. Her shadow blocked the light. If Martha had a twin, she was now right beside me. Her face was edgy, nervous. Breathing heavily, she stopped, leaned on a tree and collapsed. I was ashamed for being leery of her. The collapsed figure was in trouble. Rushing over to the tree, I watched her eyes open slightly. "It was supposed to be you," she murmured, as if in a trance.

I focused on her breathing not her words. Her pulse weakened as her skin paled, losing some of its healthy color. Knowing what to do was one thing, doing it was quite another. CPR training was something that every teacher was required to practice every year at my school. A rubber dummy reacted very differently from a breathing human being. Behind me, there was faint shouting on the trail. I barely heard it. My hands reacted by themselves, pushing and pausing in rhythm. Someone once told me if you decide to help someone and are not successful you can be sued. Pushing the daunting thought from my mind, I paused and just hoped that the crumpled figure would stretch, get up, and breathe regularly. She didn't.

"We are prepared. Let us take over." It must have been angelic medical help. Wings flapped. My own adrenalin rush quieted as the two paramedics were successful in reviving the lady. When regaining consciousness, she couldn't remember anything, not even who she was or where she was. But she remembered me.

"I tried to tell them that I wasn't you. I am not a Christian teacher," the tired lady said. "They were hunting for Sara. But I wasn't the Sara they wanted."

Hesitating momentarily, the paramedics prepared the weakened lady for her escorted ride back to one of the lodges. Strapping her carefully into a gurney, the two life savers flexed their biceps, lifted slowly, and convinced the lady that she required further medical care. Just beyond the bend in the trail, the lady shrieked, "They will find you, you know."

They were not going to find me because there was no one looking for me. The lady was delusional and just happened to be a Sara. There were probably many Saras on this trail. Relieved, I was just so glad that no one on the tour had witnessed the commotion. I was wrong.

"Sara, did you hear that lady screaming back there? What happened to her?" A winded Mr. James responded.

"She fell against a tree, and I tried to revive her. Then the medical duo showed up and stabilized her. Hyperventilation, I guess. Where is Mrs. James?"

"Then you are okay? My wife was not a trail blazer and joined a retiring group of women."

"Let's just hike." If Mr. James expected me to reveal anything more about the incident, he was thoroughly mistaken. This was probably the last hike in the last national park, and I was going to enjoy it. With Mr. James by my side, I could now refocus myself and concentrate on the beauty instead of other hikers. The professor's acquired knowledge about the park gushed out of him. The crazed lady was forgotten.

"The Grand Canyon has been here for over seventeen million years, or so they say. Indians, Sara, it is all about the Indians. Since 1200 BC, the Pueblo Indians or the Anasazi, the same tribes that inhabited the cliff dwellings, also resided in caves in this canyon."

"I just knew it. The Indian pull was so strong, the colors, the sounds, the abysses. The canyon breathes sacredness. But how in the world did they survive?"

"Well, back then, the canyon wasn't as deep. Remember the canyon's mile depth was eroded with the river and time. It is ironic that you mentioned sacred because that was exactly how the Indians felt about the canyon. It was a holy site that they made pilgrimages to."

"That must have been what that Hopi word *Ongtupqa* meant that I saw on one of the posted look out signs. Maybe the Indians feared the canyon and its awesome beauty and so worshipped it. Even today we continue to make those pilgrimages. I heard that five million people a year visit the canyon since it is probably one of the most famous natural wonders in the world. If you gaze down into the varied depths, you can hear other sounds beside the wind."

"Sara, it is a natural echo chamber. You are not superstitious are you?"

"Well, you know how the Indians felt about death. Their spirits became one with the natural world. Let's just say that I wouldn't want to be here alone at night regardless of the starry wonders."

"Remember, Sara, the Indians believed in what was around them. That was how they made sense of things. They worshiped what they hunted, what kept them alive. So naturally they believed they indwelled those creatures. At night, camping in a group might be a lot of fun."

Mr. James wanted to reassure me that there were no spirits in this canyon. A pensive woman without her husband was targeted. Mr. James just couldn't understand how my husband, a professor nonetheless, would allow me to go on a two-week bus trip by myself. He only hoped I would make it home safely and never venture off on another trip alone. Again.

Mr. James was very quiet. I didn't want to alarm him. "There must be plenty of animals in this canyon. Am I right?"

"You are right. In fact in 1903, President Theodore Roosevelt who hunted in the canyon then made the area into a game preserve. It was a good thing that he did because uranium mining and land claims wrecked havoc on both the land and animals. Later in 1919, Woodrow Wilson continued with the preservation issue and made the scenic wonder into a national park."

"What happened to all of the Indians?"

"What usually happened to them. They were ushered out one way or another. There are many tribal reservations bordering the canyon today. Water rights is a big issue right now."

The poor Indians always just tried to survive. Relaxing, I saw no totems and heard no voices. I envisioned the canyon through the Indian's eyes.

"Sara, don't move." We were resting under a scrubby tree just shade enough for the two of us. I should say the three of us. That was when I saw it.

Seeing it at a zoo, in a cage, behind bars is one thing, or watching it from the comfort of your sofa on television was another. But seeing it slithering around a tree almost ready to drop on you was horrible. I saw the snake's body wrapped around me, squeezing every ounce of air out of my body. But this was not the jungle. This was the desert. The snake wasn't even that long; it was just doing its afternoon stretches. The snake had every right to be here. It was an alarmed snake in his own habitat. But why did I have to be under it? My logic didn't soothe me at all.

"Sara, don't move a single muscle." It was the way that Mr. James said it, not what he said. The snake's colors flashed in the sun like a warning traffic light. The chanted snake rhyme my students use to sing ran through my mind. Something about a yellow fellow, but then I couldn't remember if that was the one that was poisonous. At this point, I guess it really didn't matter.

Without being detected, Mr. James cleverly edged away from the snake. Any sudden sound or movement from anyone would be unforgiving. As he looked at my face, Mr. James knew instantly that I was unfamiliar with snakes, those of the reptile family. The snake's wrapped body relaxed as it noticed my blond willowy hair that maybe resembled soft lining nest material. Any hair connection would be thwarted. A diversion was necessary. Being familiar with snakes, Mr. James remembered his pet snake that he had as a young boy. Communicating with his snake consumed him, and he quickly learned their language. It was all about the eyes. He controlled his snake's behavior with the movement of his own eyes. That was a long time ago, but he hoped it was like riding a bike. It was.

"Sara don't look at the snake." I refused to have the snake drop on me but looked away. Mr. James's command wasn't a suggestion.

It was a beginner yoga class. Mr. James's neck softly weaved from side to side as his piercing eyes fastened on to the snake's. When his neck turned to the right the snake's head followed. I expected his arms and legs to follow suit. But they didn't move. "Sara, I want you to edge forward very slowly away from the tree. Just keep inching along the ground and don't look back.

Usually I never did anything that I was ordered to do. I did just what Mr. James told me to do. After many dirty inches, I knew I was far enough away from the tree and the snake. From deep inside of me, silent sobs rose. Refusing to make a sound, I wondered how long the séance was going to last. Was Mr. James really a snake charmer? What if he couldn't charm this snake? How could I ever explain to Mrs. James that her husband was fatally wounded by a snake protecting me? I couldn't. Turning around, I saw the most amazing thing. The once determined wrapped-up snake loosened its grip and slithered down the tree disappearing into the brush. Mr. James was a professional snake charmer.

"Sara, it's over." It was over. I cried until my tears cracked. The snake charmer also cried. Emotionally, Mr. James wasn't really prepared for a total victory without a single loss. "Sara let's head back." Again, I followed without thinking. Some things you just didn't discuss. This was one of those things that would remain between just the two of us, well the three of us.

The hike back was uneventful. It was quiet, snake-less, and a rapid descent. Personally, I couldn't wait to get away from this canyon. From the moment I first stood on it, I felt its halting energy, its draining power. Weighted down, there was still something on me that shouldn't be there. The bathtub and I had a scrubbing date.

Famished, I headed for the crowded ice cream shop and ordered as though I never tasted soothing ice cream. Even as a young girl, my mother calmed my jagged fears with heaping bowls of chocolate covered ice cream. The tradition never stopped.

Exploring everything and anything was another tradition of mine. Separated only by lofty pine trees and woods, our overnight lodges were identical in every way except for their numbers. It was a forest maze and easy to get disorientated. There were long-pine-needled paths that led to each lodge. In the dark, the numbers were masked.

It had been a long while since I had walked in the starlit night with green scented pines oozing their heavy perfume. The canyon was miles away. The night air was inviting. Conversation seeped through the pines.

"If I have anything to do with it, she will go home tonight. I will go tell Mr. Hudson what happened, and I am sure that he will agree that she needs to leave. When she returns to the lodge I will tell her to pack her things and call a cab."

"First of all, you don't really know what happened. Second of all Mr. Hudson likes her. Third of all we are in a remote national park area, and there are no cabs out here."

"I don't care what I have to do but I will do whatever it takes to get her out of here. She will not be on that bus tomorrow."

Immediately, I changed directions. My spontaneous walk evolved into a tedious hike. The overheard attempt was thwarted. When I returned, no one would be awake, not even Mr. Hudson.

Their words sounded like Joel, Martha, and their sidekick Meg. But I wasn't certain. Time was on my side until I heard muffled crunching footsteps in the underbrush following me.

Once again I found myself looking over my shoulder darting back and forth on a starlit path to nowhere. One silent road led to another. I kept walking. There were no lit houses. Darkness pursued me.

"She is over there. Let's see if we can find her."

Part of me wanted to shout, "I am here come and get me," but another part didn't allow it. Without a cell phone, I was truly alone in the middle of nowhere. It was getting later and later, darker and darker with every remote road. Leon halted me.

It was stupid. I stopped. My legs ached. I was not leaving tonight. Wiping the muddy grass off my sneakers, I turned around retracing my steps back to the lodge. The echoing footsteps stopped. Exhausted, I finally located my lodge and luckily found my room. There was a neatly folded message tucked under the door requesting that I call Mr. Hudson immediately.

Mr. Hudson would wait. My fingers couldn't dial home quickly enough.

"Leon, is that you?"

"Who else would it be? What's wrong with you? You are breathing heavily. Has your asthma kicked up?"

"No, it isn't my asthma. Where were you last night? I called and called and there was nothing. I thought maybe you had fallen and were folded up in a corner somewhere."

"I tried to wait for your call, but I wasn't feeling well. Even before the cats retired, I went to bed. It won't be long now. I bet you can't wait to get off that bus and sleep in the same bed for more than one night."

"I can't. In the past two unforgiving days, so much has happened to me. A trail horse reared on me in the middle of a ravine then galloped frantically for miles. I still don't know what kept me on that horse."

"Sara, did anyone make you get on the horse?" Leon knew that I only did what I wanted to do. Forcing me to do anything was pointless.

"Well, not exactly. I wanted to go horseback riding, but it was in this Indian Reservation. There were harassing cowboys who forced me off the trail. An Indian guide loathed me because I stared at her totem. It was just all so complicated, one thing after another. None of it was supposed to happen."

"Sara, slow down. Breathe. What ever happened is over. You made it. Right? Was that totem a miniature etching of a sacred creature? Why did you stare at it?"

"That is exactly what it was. I don't really know. Like a sign post, it just caught my eye. There is more. A creepy lady fainted. A snake almost dropped on top of me. Unexplained conversations just began out of nowhere. It all started on the rim of the Grand Canyon as I hiked along the trails. Something in that Canyon couldn't rest."

"Sara it sounds like you have had an eventful two days, and you paid for this? I can think of better ways to spend your money. Seriously, I don't know why these things are happening, but there has to be a logical explanation. More than likely, I suspect some of this is exaggerated."

"I wish it were."

"Sara, don't forget that you are in Indian territory. But that shouldn't alarm you since you have always been drawn to the Indians. You know the history, the battles, the discrimination, the reservations. With your inquiring mind, I would think you would be intrigued with all of it."

"I am no longer intrigued with any of it."

"Who is banging on your door at this hour?"

"Oh that is probably Mr. Hudson checking in on me. I couldn't eat my dinner. Someone probably told him."

"Sara, you just need to relax. Slow down a bit. Answer the door before Mr. Hudson pounds a hole in it. I just don't understand why he is making a personal visit this late at night Don't stare at anyone, stay away from the snakes, and just be more aware. The trip you had to go on is almost over." Leon's last words seeped into me.

UNEXPECTED

IT WAS MORNING. I WAS still here. Bets expired. From the looks on their faces, some were quite surprised, especially Martha. Making an extra effort, I greeted her happily with my warmest grin. It was the last day in the park, in the canyon, on the river. I couldn't wait until tomorrow. But today I would relish the river rafting.

Most of us chose the outing. I didn't want to be on a raft with strangers. What I wanted didn't matter. Indiscriminately by height and weight, we were placed on the rafts.

The raft was larger than I expected. Buckled in our tightly fitting required life jackets, each one of us was positioned next to an oar lock on either side of the wobbly raft. Drifting from our posts was not permitted. We were commandeered by a retired army colonel. Our raft was the last one to leave the docking area.

Dipping into the river, our synchronized oars steered the inexperienced raft as it drifted rapidly downstream. The rapids were up ahead, churning the water this way and that. Without warning, the air changed. The energy changed. Flinging the raft like a child's toy, a torrent of water and wind slammed into us.

"Hit the bottom. Hang on to anything," the colonel hollered.

Disoriented, I felt like Dorothy in the *Wizard of Oz*. My eyes jammed shut as the rushing water pulled me into another dimension. There was no longer anything underneath me. Fighting for every breath, I kicked hard and surfaced bobbing up and down like a broken orange cork. Other broken orange corks popped up around me. Craving victims, the flashflood widened its mouth.

Someone had to do it. Someone had to take charge. Having grown up on a lake, I was probably a better swimmer than the others. Like links on a paper chain, life preservers needed to be joined together. I could do it. After all it was pure instinct, inbred. I was a teacher.

One by one encouraged arms and legs bent this way and that. Exhausted fingers reached for the nearest life preserver. The bully was uncertainty, fear. The bully was defeated individually, silently.

Against a surge of tumbling water, a flimsy human chain floated, struggling desperately. If only there were something to grab onto, overhanging debris or clumps of long wild grasses.

Then as swiftly as it started, it stopped. The spooked river spit us out of its raging mouth. In this canyon, nothing surprised me. The crazed lady's words came back to me, *"They will find you."* Something stronger stopped them. Numbed clasped hands rejoiced and grateful voices filled the dampened air. Our rafting platoon had been spared.

Limp arms cradled one another. Stronger arms lifted one another. It was a group effort. Our daunting colonel still had not surfaced. A revered silence draped the air. Two contagious thoughts grew. How were we ever going to make it out of here without a raft or without a pilot? Then both appeared out of nowhere.

Colonel Pitchard clutched parts of a ragged tee shirt, pressing down on the gushing red gash sliced across his forehead. Light headed, he swayed slightly dragging the toughened raft behind him. A stubborn trickle of blood oozed out of his mouth; he spat, cursing the river. There was no warning, not even a hint of a weather change. The colonel never would have taken this group out if there had been a possibility. His tours were his livelihood, his pride. Minor accidents were tolerated. Major casualties weren't. Once again, the Colonel tried to regain his composure, but he could hardly stand.

"It's okay," I heard myself say. "Everyone is accounted for." Bloody or not, I was just so relieved to see him. I almost hugged him. No longer did I feel wholly responsible for these bewildered rafters. The colonel gazed at me, studying me. His body couldn't catch up with his mind.

"Everyone made it?"

"In one form or another, mostly bruises but no apparent broken bones. How did you happen to salvage the raft?"

"Somehow I was pinned under it in an air pocket. These army-like rafts are heavy duty, almost indestructible. They can easily suffocate you but are hardly ever punctured. The oars need to be found. Well intended arms won't make it. There are whirling rapids below that can only be navigated with oars."

Listening to the colonel, I even felt responsible for him. His words tried so hard to convince but he was weakened and his heart wasn't in it.

"We will find the oars. There are no other rafts in sight. Are we that far behind the others?"

"You know what this is, don't you? Not everybody makes it in a flashflood. We will look for survivors as we continue down the river." Tears welled up in the colonel's tired eyes as he drifted away.

"We all made it. I am certain that the others made it as well." The colonel no longer listened, no longer tried. His legs could no longer hold him. He succumbed, collapsing on the grassy bank beneath him. I never thought that anything might happen to the colonel. He just seemed so commanding, so invincible, but he wasn't. I was right back where I started from, not wanting to be in charge but someone had to do it.

Luckily, the missing oars were not splintered, were in one piece, and fit stubbornly back into their designated slots. The seating arrangement changed. Those who could row rowed; the others huddled together propping up the fading colonel who barely spoke. Pain was everywhere. I focused on the rapids that lay before us. The plan was simple enough, keep the raft balanced and get through the churning rapids without overturning. Hawk-eyed, we scavenged for survivors along the way. There weren't any. I didn't know if that were a good sign or a bad sign. I didn't want to know.

This was not my first time on a raft. But this was my first time on such a wide river cordoned off by stretched up reddish, orange limestone cliffs. And to think yesterday I was gazing contently at this tiny etched in river. If only I had known what might happen. I should have known. Gazing into the chilled river, I was keenly aware that no one could fall overboard a second time. No one would make it out alive. Right now, rubbed splotchy arms and legs were barely working.

Age was random, experience wasn't. But now even experience meant nothing. The colonel steered this river thousands of times, it only took one time to be defeated.

"Keep the colonel awake. Whatever you do, just keep talking to him. You have to prevent him from going into shock." No one answered, but I heard encouraged voices nudge him. What some of the others said was deafening.

"Do you really think that we are going to make it?" asked the chilled couple who shook together in the bottom of the raft next to my knees. "Without a trained instructor, I mean what chance do we really have?" Throwing their deafening comment overboard, I no longer remained silent.

"Our chance is what we make it. Like anything else that happens randomly in life, if we work together we can do it, instructor or not. We know what we need to do, so let's just get it done."

"You are, Sara, aren't you? From what I have heard, you sound just like her." I didn't know if it were a compliment or not. I didn't care. I didn't bother to answer. It didn't matter. Oar strides steadied, strengthened. Refocused, our effort soared.

"We are going to make it. If it is the last thing that I do on this earth, this raft is going to get through these rapids without flipping over. Everyone including the colonel will get out of this raft with their own two feet and walk on dry land," one of the rowers behind me bellowed. Mr. Wearin spoke just in time. The rapids hit us hard.

"Hard to the right. Keep your weight steady. Keep the oars deep in the water." He had taken over. Mr. Wearin knew boats. He was a sailor. "Veer to the left. Pull the oars back in the water in a circular motion. Hang on! This is the worst of it. Focus on your oars. Keep them level. Whatever you do, don't let go of your oars." In this shaky raft, there was heightened spirit. Drenched with river spray, determined faces didn't flinch. Whitened fingers didn't loosen. Breathing quickened. If we were ever going to break through the white water, it was now.

Whispering, the colonel groaned. "Watch out for the drop." It was almost too late. Camouflaged behind a low hanging jagged rock, the drop completely turned the tumbling raft around. It was an out of control Ferris wheel at a cursed circus. Fate showed its hand. We showed ours. Instinctively, weary hands reached out to one another anchoring arms and legs. Persevering, our pride puckered up. No one really believed that the raft didn't toss us out like toy soldiers. The rapids waned. Inhaling victory, our goal neared. Getting off this river alive penetrated every thought.

About a mile in front of us, there was a floating object that clung to the bedraggled shoreline. Edging closer and closer, we heard ragged rafters crying out desperately for help. Not everyone defeated the spinning rapids. Their stunned guide lost his footing and was shoved violently overboard. Terror was a cancerous growth that spread among those who were left behind.

Silence poured out of us. It was the worst scenario that anyone could have possibly imagined. Our own damaged guide was experiencing stages of hibernation. No one really knew what to do. What we had to do was find the guide. With quivering, cold lips we agreed that all of us would make it off this river or none of us would. Again, pride tugged at my tired heart. Colonel Pritchard raised his weary head.

"Check the bushes, the grasses, the branches. The river is wide. Look for colors, anything that moves." With that said, the colonel closed his heavy eyes and lay his weary head back down on the raft's bottom. That was the plan? But how? Turning away, I didn't want anyone to see my cringing disbelief.

Thrusting my hands into my pockets, I then found the way to execute the plan, my trusty binoculars. Not wasting a minute, I yanked them out and scanned. Usually I focused on birds, but this was no different. Refocusing the lenses, I panned up and down the river's bank and suddenly witnessed two human hands struggling. Almost dropping my binoculars, I gasped.

"There he is, there he is over there." One after another anxious fingers clutched the binoculars wanting to witness the whereabouts of the missing guide. Triumphant cries, weakened cheers, and questions rang out. Traversing the river would take a tremendous amount of energy, determination, and mostly luck. Who in their right mind would volunteer for this kamikaze mission?

"I will go. So will I." A resounding cry arose from the huddled figures. Even though most of them could hardly move, both men and women volunteered. Again, Mr. Wearin, the outspoken sailor presided, choosing only those who could hold a steady oar. His eyes swept right past me. Obviously, women were not his priority. A true sailor but I intervened. I was not going to be overlooked.

"Count me in," I announced. Barely acknowledging me, Mr. Wearin barely made room for me in the raft. Leaving my binoculars in other hands, I took my seat wishing I had stayed behind. The water churned relentlessly as we attempted to get across. It should have been a certain death ride, but it wasn't. There was something in that raft that pulled us across safely. Reaching the other side, we sensed it; we knew it.

When we located the helpless water-logged guide, he just gave up and succumbed to the river. Heaving his heavy, water-soaked body into the raft, we watched breathlessly as Mr. Wearin softly pushed on his back. Spitting up fountains of water, the guide momentarily opened his grateful, water-clogged eyes then slumped into oblivion. Another guide down.

Across the river, there was a celebration as distant cheers urged us on. The chilled air bit into our hands and faces. Without hesitating, Mr. Wearin took off his jacket and covered the guide's numbed figure. The guide's circulation was critical. Rubbing his arms and legs continuously, I was determined to bring any healthy color back into his hypothermic body. Sadly by varying degrees, we were all hypothermic. Rowing back was easier, quicker. We had already proven ourselves.

Once again, the two salvaged rafts were equally filled and balanced by weight. Some of the rattled rafters changed rafts. It really didn't make a difference which one you were in. Neither had a functioning guide. The water calmed. Relentlessly, the cold seeped into us. Hope was beyond us.

Mr. Wearin read my mind. Abruptly, he ordered everyone out of the rafts. "Roll on the grass and don't stop." No one even questioned him. We rolled. It was intoxicating warmth. "Stuff the grass under your jackets, in your shirts, anywhere and everywhere." We stuffed. Looking like barnyard scarecrows, we bundled into the waiting rafts.

The rafts were not given an opportunity to flip over again. With some discovered rope, Mr. Wearin tethered the rafts together to prevent any further mishaps. All would really make it or none would. Further instructions were given and enforced. No one under any circumstances could stand up. Oars would not be dropped. Alternate groups of designated rowers were set up to give others rest. Every ounce of energy was used. But was it enough?

When we departed from the dock, our river excursion was supposed to last about two hours. Already, we had spent twice that amount of time without going very far. No one knew how much river lay ahead of us. The proverbial saying, "The glass was half empty or half full," applied. On our parts, it was a deliberate, conscious effort. Warm, stuffed grass kindled shreds of hope.

Our passionate conversation was not about mouthwatering foods. Instead we fantasized about favorite warm clothes: flannel shirts, cozy warm-up suits, woolen sweaters, heavy socks, and mittens, lots of mittens. Adjustable heaters and kindling fires were drooled over. Maybe there was a chance to get off this uncertain river.

Many minutes passed. Hands tightened, fingers slipped, no one could hold on to the oars. Encouraging words were no longer heard from Mr. Wearin. The rafts were not going to row themselves. Regardless of the rules, some of the women crumbled and cried. Calloused men with runaway tears streaked across their drawn faces joined their wives. Outwitting us, the cold won.

Then like a mirage on a desert's horizon, two motor-powered rafts appeared out of nowhere heading straight for us. No one believed what they saw; no one cared until we actually heard the roar of the motors. It was a scene from a writer's heart. Evidently spared, we were going to be rescued. Disbelief and thankfulness poured out of every mouth. The rescuers hurried expertly, wasting no time.

"Everyone just take it easy. Everything is going to be fine. We have blankets, coffee, hot chocolate, and we are going to get you out of here. You will not have to row with another oar on another raft unless of course you ever want to." His humor was defining as heaping cups of steaming coffee were placed in our frozen hands. My whole body felt as though I was skiing underdressed in twenty degree weather. I quickly got off the mountain and snuggled into an army blanket.

The ride back was a blur. Each one of us suffered, some more than others. The rescuers did their best to restore clarity. Being restored, I wondered why we started out with oars instead of motors in the first place. It was probably to savor every delightful aspect of being on the river. Every delightful aspect on the river almost destroyed us.

True to our vows, we all did make it, even the fallen guides. I thought for sure that they would give up their guiding oars, but they didn't. In fact when both of their own feet carried them out of the raft, they were only concerned about tomorrow's schedule. Any one of our guiding oars was removed swiftly and permanently.

Waving frantically, a paled, exhausted Mr. Hudson half stood leaning on the end of the landing dock looking as if he saw a ghost. With all of the conflicting reports, Mr. Hudson envisioned the worst. One hour, the rafts were declared lost with no hope of survival, the next hour some hope was restored as the flash flood waned. Nothing concrete was ever projected. Up until an hour ago, it was anyone's guess.

Mr. Hudson unraveled like a loosely tied shoelace. The loved ones left behind stung like a hornet's nest. Demanding action they would do something if he didn't. The cry of law suits prevailed. Forget about the expected end of the trip tips, Mr. Hudson would be lucky if he wasn't sued for everything he owned, which wasn't much. Accusations:

"How come he did not know that a flash flood was imminent? Why wasn't a rescue party organized immediately? Why had he subjected all of them to such trauma? Why? Why? Why?"

How in the world would he explain to his devoted wife and two young sons that he was calling from a jail cell and charged with negligence? If anyone were negligent, it would be the rafting company's executives. Regardless, it was his tour. Ultimately, he was responsible.

Grabbing the raft's attached ropes, Mr. Hudson eased the rafts into the landing area. Witnessing the uncovered trauma, his heart sank. Blankets dropped, revealing stiffly frozen, crunchy, clothes. Hands, arms, and legs were aflame, red, sore. Paralyzed eyes gazed coldly at him. He was going to jail. He should go to jail. The lawsuits didn't bother him. There would be no paid representation, no attorney. There was nothing to protect.

"Mr. Hudson, please help me, my feet are stuck." It was Sara. "It is so good to see you Mr. Hudson. I never really thought that I would ever see you again." I just fell into his arms as other arms reached out and grabbed tottering figures. Compassion smothered resentment.

Mr. Hudson forced himself to ask. "Sara did anyone not...."

"Everyone made it." If locked up, at least now Mr. Hudson would have a cleared conscience.

There was no time to lose. Crunchy, cold clothes were snake skins that were quickly shed for warm, layers of warmth. Ambulances cordoned off the parking lot and were standing at attention. The fallen would be escorted to the nearest hospital, which was a ways a way. Fingers swelled. Ankles puffed. Healthy arms and legs scurried to help failing arms and legs regain color and feeling. Warm clothes and warm voices nurtured healing. No one wanted to go to the hospital. No one had to except the two battered guides who were in and out of consciousness. For the rest of us, one traumatized ride was enough for one day.

Except for one specific corner, I never before witnessed so much caring in such a remote parking lot. No one wanted to let anyone out of their sight. Huddled in that one corner were Mr. Hudson, the park rangers, and personnel from the rafting company. As if on cue, one crisp suit arrived after another. Intense conversation rallied. Mr. Hudson lost all objectivity. He wanted answers, and he wanted them now.

Hurriedly, someone handed Mr. Hudson a cell phone. Walking a few steps in the opposite direction, he turned and stopped ranting. Mrs. Hudson's high-pitched frantic voice halted his anger. His wife didn't know if he were on the tormented rafts or not. For hours, she had been desperately trying to reach him. A news crew who just happened to be in the area documented and televised the flashflood's wrath. The publicity was unwanted, unnerving. His wife's voice pulled him back to reality. A jail cell was not waiting for him. He didn't even know if he still had a job or if he even wanted it. He did know that he would keep this documented tour group safe, warm, and well fed, returning them to Las Vegas any way he could.

As stinging limbs thawed, survivors became celebrities. Reporters wanted every gruesome detail, every chilling thought, every desperate feeling. Hearts emptied. Everyone's version was slightly different. It didn't really matter. Most of it sounded like a ghastly nightmare to wake up from.

Touted a hero by many, Mr. Wearin burst with pride. Lawsuits were forgotten as reunited couples called their loved ones, assuring them that they were warm and breathing. Everything told me to call Leon, but his altering rage would make Mr. Hudson's heightened abruptness insignificant. When I spoke to Leon, there had to be calmness. I was anything but calm.

The reporters were long gone. When we finally reached the chalet, our closeness began to blur. There was nothing left to say. Suddenly, privacy was important. Each one of us eagerly disappeared back into our own life. Thankfully, it was the last night in this canyon, and the very last night of this grueling bus tour. Las Vegas waited for us.

When I piled on another sweater, another pair of socks, and perched near my room's tiny toasty radiator heater, my every fantasy was fulfilled. I had everything that I ever wanted except peace of mind.

The call. Leon was way ahead of me. The phone rang. There was an urgent telegram for me at the desk. I was shocked that a telegram could be delivered to this remote area, to this cabin. It must have been brought by a fearless mountain goat and his devoted herder. I didn't even have to open the telegram. Volcanic anger seeped through it. Leon was beside himself and purchased an airline ticket. He would personally bring me back in one piece or however many pieces there were. My shame reared its ugly head. Guilt raced through every cell in my body.

How did he know? Leon didn't usually watch much of the news. The daily violence portrayed was never worth his time. Did everyone know? An informed someone who did watch the news must have alarmed him. I loved this someone. This someone patrolled my heart always knowing when I was in trouble.

I could hear my mother's relentless cry. "Find her, find her, Leon, you have got to find out what happened to her."

Again the phone rang. "We just had to know that you were okay. You never should have gone on this trip alone. I know that I urged you to go. I was wrong." My mother's voice quivered like a bowl of un-jelled lime Jell-o. In the background I heard, "Let me talk to her, let me talk to her." My father's voice steadied.

"We are very proud of you for just getting through it. After all you are a fish in the water and have inherited most of my genes not to mention your mother's stubbornness."

My mother's cries deafened me. To comfort her was the only thing that mattered to me.

Knotted with fear, Leon's voice quickened. "Did you get the telegram? Why haven't you called? I thought you were missing, drifting facedown somewhere on that pounding river. Your dad and I almost hired a helicopter to go look for you." Again shame was thrust in my face.

"I just got back to the lodge and——"

"Sara, I don't really care what you are doing just that you are doing something, anything. Worried doesn't convey the way I feel. Scared doesn't. Regretful rage comes close. I just couldn't bear the thought of losing you to a chilly impersonal river. How could I possibly explain it to anyone especially your parents? None of it makes any sense. Since you will return shortly, your dad made me cancel the flight. But if you still want a private escort, I can leave now. From the beginning Sara, this trip was doomed. I just want you to know that once you do get back home, I will not let you out of my sight, except of course to get groceries." This was a lover's voice, the rage had softened.

"Leon, a private escort would be excessive and impractical. I am almost home. And I promise that I won't leave the house except of course for groceries. Maybe it took the perilous rafting to wake me up, knowing that everything could be taken away from me at any moment without warning. Please don't be upset. Just try to keep the cats calm and reassure my mother that I will make it home shortly. My mother needs a hug. My father probably doesn't."

The day wore itself out. I wore myself out. Reassuring the three people that I loved most in the world, I suddenly became chilled again. Their warm loving words clamored into my soul, opening up home. Was it really over? Was I really off the raft? Was I warm? Had I survived? Heaving sighs of pure panic, shock, and utter relief, I tumbled forward on the sofa. Part of me would always be on that raft waiting to be rescued.

BROKEN CHAINS

THE MORNING'S CASCADING SUNLIGHT WARMED my room, waking me up earlier than usual. Piled on top of me were numerous blankets. Like an enclosed mummy, I quickly crawled out of my tomb. Mercilessly, I was tossed back and forth on the raft all night long. My mind ached more than my body. Unable to shake yesterday's calamity, I just couldn't seem to get a grip on right now. Once I returned home, I was certain Leon would annihilate it. Most of my summer still lay ahead of me before I had to return to school. But I had no inkling how long it would take me to recover from this trip.

I visualized Las Vegas—jumping off the bus for the very last time—grabbing my suitcase and repressing most of what happened during the last two weeks except the beautiful scenery. Remembering Mr. Hudson's tip money, I realized that I only had ten dollars left to my name. I would just have to figure something out.

At breakfast, Mr. Hudson acted strangely, dotting on each one of us, talking about anything and everything, and giving compliments that weren't warranted. Afterwards, he personally escorted most of us to the bus making sure that our luggage was stowed away properly in the side bins. Mrs. Hudson probably instructed him not to let anyone wander out of his periphery for any reason. He didn't.

Except for a few hellos, no one really had much to say or so I thought. But when the bus's engine roared, so did the negative comments. Mr. Hudson always sat up front so he heard none of it. I wished that I heard none of it. Like plastic to be used again, negative energy recycled itself, encouraging others to spread its foulness.

The flash flood was nature's wrath, nature's will. No one detected it. No one knew. No one was blamed except Mr. Hudson. Slanderous evaluations were going to be sent in to the touring company. Mr. Hudson would never direct another tour. I disagreed.

"I just want everyone to know how thankful I am that no one was seriously hurt yesterday. All of us should be so grateful that we were rescued successfully. I can't wait to make my sentiments known in writing." Disbelief echoed up and down the rows. "Anyone who thinks differently should re-examine the circumstances." The swirling condemnations halted. No one bothered to look at me. It was quiet when Mr. Hudson made his aisle walk through.

"Who does she think she is telling me how I should or shouldn't feel? I didn't spend all of this money to end up in a hospital or worse."

"Did you go to the hospital?"

"Well, I could have."

"But you didn't." Someone picked up where I left off. Sides were chosen; opinions were expressed quietly with decency and respect. It turned into a counseling session and that is probably what everyone needed anyway.

"The once close-knit couples disbanded. You never would have known that all of us had been traveling together for two consecutive weeks on a bus. Friendly outgoing individuals were quiet. Ever since Percy's fallout with Crazy Horse, her desire to commune with others was gone. She hardly even spoke to me. Ignoring one another, Martha and Joel seemed happier apart. Now, sitting by himself on the bus, Joel seemed more content than ever. He and his camera were once again inseparable. Martha's magnetic pull on Meg ceased. Bullying no longer united them. The Australian couple endeared themselves to one another instead of to everyone else. Relationships made during the first week were now obsolete. Two long confining weeks indiscriminately changed people.

Some changed for the better. Mr. James and Mr. Morrow became nicer as the days passed. I don't know what I would have done without them. A true educator, Mr. James and his endearing snake dance were tucked away in my mind forever. Mr. Morrow's friendliness covered his wife's reluctance. It was nice to listen to someone who knew everything about most things. Maybe even a soul had been altered. Joel said that he would think about going to church and reading a Bible. That in itself was worth all the harassment from his endearing wife.

I realized that I also changed. I was no longer leery of strangers. Anything imaginable already happened to me. My sore ignorant eyes were opened day after day after day. Witnessing the best and the worst of human nature, I was proud of the best and shamed at the worst. The injustice of the Indian plight still sickened me. Their beliefs and spiritual sacrifice gnawed at me. The determined bare back feathered warriors and their painted ponies would never leave me.

Not everything changed me for the better. I wasn't given a chance to choose. The demented lady's parting comments in the Grand Canyon, *"They will find you, you know,"* still jolted me. Yesterday, during the rafting turmoil, I clearly heard only those around me. Those were the voices that I focused on. Somehow, the danger had separated me from the unwanted voices. Their spiritual hideouts now hid them. I couldn't have been more wrong.

As the canyon faded in the distance, I felt a tremendous burden, a heavy bag of reddish boulders, tumble from my shoulders. I made it out alive. No one could change that. Sinking deep into my seat, I enjoyed the quiet, allowing my mind to slow, unwind, and relax. After a few hours, I awoke, refreshed. The raft no longer harassed me. I doubted whether any of us slept at all last night.

NOT BACK YET

ANTICIPATION ROSE AS LAS VEGAS cordoned in on us. I never saw so many people watching their watches, including Mr. Hudson. Mr. Footsin, the bus driver and a Vietnam veteran, did his best to entertain us with grueling war stories and questionable jokes. Heads bobbed every which way curtailing the jokes. A stoic Mr. Hudson didn't even try to entertain us. There were no stops along the way. Our speed seemed to gradually increase every hour. A watched pot never boils. I seemed to be the only one who watched. We boiled. Not being fond of speed, I knew that it only took an instant for an accident. Smelling it before seeing it, I choked on the stench of rancid oil. My lungs ached as I gulped in air. Others gasped. We hit. A sprawled tanker overturned. A thick oozing sludge of oil spilled, covering the highway. Cars slid out of control.

"Hit the floor!" Mr. Footsin yelled, scrambling to keep the bus balanced. Hit the floor? Maybe I wasn't going to make it off this bus alive. Sleep was assaulted. Heads rolled. Knocked from his seat, Mr. Hudson sprawled Indian style in the aisle. "Pretend that you are in a bunker. We are in this bunker together." A bunker? Mr. Footsin's flashback nearly did him in. He saw soldiers, ragged, bloodied, desperate. Forcing himself to ease up on the breaks, Mr. Footsin tried to veer oft the highway, missing the mangled cars ahead of him that looked like connected dominos in an unfinished game.

Mr. Flinn, a war veteran himself, recognized the haunting look that stared back at him in the oversized rearview mirror. He was seated right behind Mr. Footsin and didn't take his eyes off the mirror. Edging closer to Mr. Footsin, he calmly talked to the haunted soldier, easing him back to reality. Escaping certain disaster, the bus lunged off the highway. Clogged with thick black smelly oil, the brakes no longer worked. Trees lunged at us knowing we trespassed. Terrain was ripped open as the bus's oversized wheels gouged out long furrows in the ground. Surely someone would know how to stop this bus. No one did. Twisting through the trees, Mr. Footsin did his best to slow the bus as we approached a slopping ravine. It was a huge drop. If the bus didn't flip over, it would be surreal. If the bus did flip over, none of us would survive. The mangled cars on the highway would look intact compared to the crushed bus at the bottom of this ravine.

"The escape hatch. What about the escape hatch?"

"Ram it open or get out of the way." What I heard didn't make any sense. Were people really going to jump off of the bus? Then it made perfect sense. You might break a few bones but at least you would be alive. Remaining on the bus was witnessing your own death certificate. Mr. Hudson no longer controlled the bus. It was out of his jurisdiction. His face was paler than his egg-white cap.

Someone yelled, "It is the raft all over again. But without the water." That comment assaulted us or united us. Adrenalin saturated the air. Much to my horror, the hatch was forced opened with a crow bar and jumpers lined up. Goodbyes were forgotten. There wasn't time.

Mr. Footsin was in the fight of his life, mentally and physically. He was back in the concentration camp and decided to escape. There really was no escape, but he would die trying. Mr. Footsin was very aware that only he could stop the runaway bus. Mr. Footsin jolted the steering wheel hard to the left and slammed on the brake pedals with both of his feet. It was target practice as the bus veered headlong into the middle of an unsuspecting pine grove. The pines tugged at the bus, halting it. Then the strangest thing happened. Jumpers jumped. I jumped. Mr. Hudson jumped. Each one of us jumped except Mr. Footsin. It was a right of passage. It was so freeing knowing that you could jump if you had to. Of course, it wasn't exactly the same, the bus wasn't moving, but it didn't seem to matter.

Mr. Footsin no longer saw soldiers surrounding him. But what he saw alarmed him even more. Why did everyone jump out of the escape hatch at the back of the bus? Had he overlooked something? Steadying himself, he got up and opened the dented bus doors, exiting the bus the way you were supposed to. Cheers of pure joy filled his ears as the tourist chorus sang "You are the Jolly Good Fellow." He had stopped the runaway, cheating death once again.

Mr. Footsin was no longer an ordinary man, just a bus driver. For a few minutes, he was a hero and savored every blissful minute. The monotonous hours that he spent commandeering buses for days on end vanished. Gripping him since the war's end, his uncontrolled flashbacks even quieted. Eventually, gleeful euphoria gave way to reality. Even if the bus wanted to move, it was not going another inch.

There were two choices: wait for help which would never come or hike out of the woods with our own two feet. With our fearless leader before us, a band director leading a parade, Mr. Hudson orchestrated our hike through the woods. One way was as good as another as we headed back towards the highway. Our luggage was all that remained behind. No one really cared. It was safe where it was. Who would find it, let alone want it? Maybe only a determined raccoon.

Walking in the quilted deep pine needles was a concern. Layers and layers of crunchy needles gave way to small open fields where natural wildlife thrived. Surely something lived under all off the decomposing needles, but no one really wanted to know. Listening for traffic noises, bird yelps, and water sounds, Mr. Hudson hurried along driven by instinct. Streams usually led somewhere, hopefully out of this deepening forest. Reaching civilization before nightfall was a must. After dark, there would be unwanted sounds: forlorn cries of bears, wolves, and coyotes staking claims on prey and territory. You didn't want to be either.

Part of Mr. Hudson wondered if he could still do it. Would he have to? As a fourteen-year-old boy scout on his first primitive camping trip, Mr. Hudson still smelled and felt the coaxed flames of his first fire. If there were no fire, this darkened forest with its animals would not forgive.

With wear and tear smudged on our faces, many lagged behind, already exhausted from yesterday's rafting ordeal. A ten- mile hike with uneven terrain was not part of today's itinerary. Collapsing, foot warriors sprawled on the soft pine needles refusing to move.

"Mr. Hudson, you need to stop, or no one will be able to follow you." Mr. Hudson's silence gripped Mr. Footsin. "Just turn around, there isn't anyone behind us."

"We have to get out of these woods before nightfall."

"I know what we have to do, but that doesn't mean that we are going to be able to accomplish it. There has to be another plan. Fire, a cleared area and luck, tons of luck. Any kind of water would provide fish and maybe berries.

"Boy Scouts?"

"And Eagle Scouts."

An Eagle Scout. Mr. Hudson felt rushing assurance. The night no longer tore at him. Sitting down on untouched pine needles, Mr. Hudson thought of her. Another broken promise to his beloved wife. They would not return tonight. Blocked by mountains, a cell phone's call was a wish more than a reality. Loving someone so much had its consequences.

While the sun dropped in the sky, our feet dropped on the trail. The remaining miles would have to wait. Like a spell, mutiny cowered in the air. Some wanted to continue, most couldn't. If anything happened to anyone, Mr. Hudson was still responsible. A few determined men prompted Mr. Footsin to lead, but his war flashbacks overruled. The group remained intact. The boy scouts took charge.

Once again, those fourteen-year-old boys were tested. With shadows widening, the cold seeped in. Branches for kindling were stacked by the pit. Wide eyes watched as Mr. Hudson and Mr. Footsin rubbed sticks together. But primitive fire was overtaken with intervention when a forgotten lighter was accidentally found.

As if making a huge oversized eagle's nest, Mr. Footsin and others hauled out brush and feathered the cleared ground with pine needles, making it ready for nesting. Blackberry bushes covered the perimeter, and royal purple ripened fruit was ravished. It was a fruit pie without the crust.

Once the fires danced, childhood spiritual songs rose up like channeled smoke. In the mix, there were also forgotten girl scouts. Star-laden clusters were sought out, identified, and discussed. The night sky was an obsession. Softness closed in and eyelids shut. What could have been a certain disaster turned into a celebrated evening of natural wonders. Claiming a corner of the nest, I rearranged my arms and legs, covering myself with needles.

A deep throaty cry ripped through the cool night air. My legs cramped with tension. The fire's flames had relented, and only a few stubborn glowing embers remained. Then I saw what no one wanted to see at night, a bear's huge towering outline. Thick with blackberry juice, the air enticed the approaching animal. My corner was further away from the others. Most of the curled figures were nestled closer to the center of the clearing. A deep midsummer's night dream encircled the nest. No one stirred, not even the boy scouts. The volunteer watch guard posts were abandoned. The hunched figure knew it.

Fire was life. Reaching the nearest pit, my legs gave way after I crawled in pain towards the neon signposts, the glowing embers. Never did I take my eyes off the commanding silhouette. Staring, I ripped up pieces of bark adding twigs to the fire, knowing that any minute I would be assaulted, disfigured beyond recognition. With one paw swipe, my middle-aged life would be rudely taken away. Why had I put the group's safety and well being first? I wished I had woken someone, anyone so I didn't have to suffer alone. From behind, deep breathing refocused me. It wasn't from a bear.

"Sara, don't be afraid." Mr. Footsin had awoken with one of his flashbacks and then realized it was real. "I know bears. Stoking the fire was a good start, but it will take more than that. We need a diversion. If nothing else, the bear must be lead away from the group. Where there is one bear, there is usually another. If I don't return, tell Mr. Hudson what happened. He will know what to do."

If you don't return, I couldn't believe what he just said. Mr. Footsin must still be half asleep. But before I could intervene, he grabbed a stick, thrust it into the flames, waved it in the air like a death banner, turned and blended into the woods.

"Mr. Hudson, wake up, it's Mr. Footsin."

"That crazy old fool. He has done it this time. A bear, was it really a bear?" The boy scout in him churned. "Quickly, wake up everyone. Make some fire torches." Mr. Footsin, one of the best bus drivers in the business was not going to be bear fodder. Stampeding, Mr. Hudson's nerves raced as he grabbed a lit torch and headed into the woods determined to find Mr. Footsin before the bear did. Bravery ousted fear when one by one other men awoke, quickly grabbed torches and followed one another into the deepening woods. From one end to the other, a scattered line of fire lamps lit up the woods. Others couldn't or wouldn't move and huddled by one of the many fires, which now lit up the night like an opera's spotlight. The curtain had already lifted.

It was humbling knowing that some might not return. It was humbling that some cared enough to try.

"Sara, you look white as a caliche road in this light." It was Mr. James whose wife held on to his arm as if her life depended on it. "With all of this commotion, I am certain that the bear will desist and move on. If I were a bear, I would." Mrs. James couldn't take another step and gushed endless tears like a cracked geyser.

"It's not just the bear. It is everything that has happened on this trip. What else do we have to endure before we can get home? It just isn't fair. This was suppose to be a soothing anniversary celebration not a winding obstacle course." I didn't know what to say, but I knew that crying was contagious and wasn't going to help anything.

"Mrs. James, sometimes things happen without any warning. Luckily, we had a warning. The bear could have easily mauled anyone at anytime but didn't. With that said, the geyser stopped. Mrs. James appreciated Sara's calmness and level headedness. Her raging selfishness embarrassed her.

"I guess I was just overwhelmed. Comforting the other women will be good therapy for me. Sara, thank you."

"We all have unnerving moments, but it is what we do with them that counts."

A significant part of me wanted to grab a torch adding a light to the jagged line of distant torches. But I knew that I was needed here at camp. Much of the confused fear lingered in worn, elderly faces. They just couldn't comprehend what just happened.

"The bear was for you and you alone." Grabbing a lit torch, I chased the taunting sounds coming from within the woods. If the bear were for me, let it come and get me and not the others. Groaning pine boughs snapped under my feet and slapped my calves and thighs. One way or the other, I would find where those words came from. Nothing would stop me. Deeper and deeper I sunk into the woods. A cry of defiance rose inside me.

"If you want me come and get me. I am right here. Waiting." The deep woods didn't answer. But I heard carried conversation from all around me.

"Whoever it is, something dreadful must have happened. Who else could possibly be in here by themselves? Hurry. It came from over there. Who is it? It's Sara. Sara, Sara, why are you screaming? It's okay, there is nothing here. The bear is gone Sara, your screams saved us. We were lost. You turned us back around with your outcry."

"I did? No one was mauled?"

"Sara, the bear wasn't really after anyone; it was just hungry and thought there was more at camp than blackberry juice." It was an exhausted Mr. Footsin, leaning against a deadened propped up stump.

"Let's just get back to camp before others follow after you," said Mr. Hudson anxious for this all to be behind them. It was too late. Witnessing my dramatic departure, a search party frantically attacked the woods trying in vain to find me. Everyone helped. No one wanted to be left behind. That was how the rest of the night went; one group looked for another group until all were finally accounted for and back at base camp watching the sun peak over the stoic hills. Toasting the sunrise, we envisioned imaginary glasses of chilled champagne and were thankful to be warm, breathing, and alive.

What happened next was nothing less than extraordinary. A helicopter with a radiating sound system flew over head, assuring us that people were searching for us. Help was on its way.

One of the older ladies shrieked, "Don't go, don't go. Please don't leave us."

Amazingly, the helicopter hovered then circled back around landing bull's eye right in the center of our clearing. Two young pilots slid out of the cockpits hauling a container of much-needed water bottles and a few choice candy bars.

One of the pilots hurried over to a relieved, weeping Mrs. Miles. "You reminded me of my mother. I just had to come back and make sure that you were okay."

The water tasted better than champagne, and the shared chocolate bars like broiled steak. The broken down bus was found by an unsuspecting hiker. Our luggage was still intact. No one could believe that we were the very same televised tour group who had battled the infamous rapids. Once again, our families were alerted regarding our continued demise. The pilots radioed a second time for help but from their own kind. No one wanted to get back on another bus. We didn't. This too was an unexpected addition to the itinerary, but it was by far the most exciting part of the trip.

Before long there was a flutter in the air like a platoon of dragonflies as helicopters buzzed base camp landing safely one by one. We were scooped up like apples ready for harvest and whisked away towards Las Vegas. I happened to be boxed with Percy and Mr. Footsin who helped Percy on board since she was unsteady. Since her traumatized fall, Percy changed and was unable to handle anything that looked, tasted, or smelled of stress. This included all three. This trip had altered many of us, some more than others. Bombarded by extreme and difficult circumstances, each one of us embraced camouflage.

With Percy's edginess and Mr. Footsin's disorientation, there was little left to do but enjoy the ride. The loud slicing of the helicopter blades unleashed Mr. Footsin's burdened mind, and wild night visions of war helicopter missions filled our senses. The more I heard, the less I listened. Even with Percy's constant sighing, Mr. Footsin was relentless and couldn't or wouldn't stop. I just hoped that Mr. Footsin didn't become so anxious that he opened the flimsy door and jumped out.

More than concerned, the young pilot overtly changed the subject and shared visions of his own missions, day rescues. The air lightened; and curiously, Mr. Footsin fell asleep. Relieved, Percy and I listened contentedly to our headphones. Giving all his attention to the panel controls, the focused pilot just wanted to land safely and make that long overdue promised call to his mother. He would not neglect her again.

Like blackened geese, the helicopters followed one another in a V-like formation.

After about an hour, the whirling blades slowed to a lower hum as we descended. There was little formality; nothing like a commercial airplane. Our belts were never unbuckled and there were no tables to tuck back in position. But what was there amazed me. There was nothing on the runway. Flight paths were abandoned. No aircraft of any size was lifting off or landing. As far as the eye could see there were onlookers, thousands of them on both sides of the runway. Anonymity had escaped us.

As if returning from a top secret military mission, the helicopters landed one by one maintaining the V-formation. No one hurried. No one got out of line. The onlookers probably expected dignitaries and heads of states, not a band of bedraggled tourists. But they were here for us. As it should be, Mr. Hudson was in the first helicopter, and got out first. When his weary feet met the runway, a loud drum roll met his ears. Mr. Hudson's flimsy baton was passed to a real live band director who applauded him with his band's mighty sound. It was a warrior's welcome.

In one way or another, I guess we were all partly warriors. We survived. Many circulated oversized envelopes were chocked full with tips for Mr. Hudson. Against flashfloods, oil spills, broken down buses, and unforgiving wilderness, he promised to get us back to Las Vegas, and it was exactly what he did. Mr. Hudson deserved so much more than anything that could be put into an envelope.

With our feet firmly planted on concrete, we smiled weakly, waved, and waited for each helicopter to unload. Quickly departing, the V-formation faded effortlessly into the distance as our own goodbyes surfaced. There were only a few on my list: Mr. James and his weakened wife, Mr. Moles and his jealous wife, Percy, obnoxious Meg, and a few others who started friendly conversations out of curiosity or boredom. A sense of civility crept in knowing that we would never again be a part of this jinxed traveling group for any reason. Then we scattered like bird seed thrown into the wind searching for loved ones.

Mentally I jumped for joy knowing the trip was finally over. When I realized others headed for that same taxi, my celebration was short-lived. Cramming myself into the hotel taxi, I was squished in between others from our group. Like a posted unwritten rule there was no conversation in the taxi. As if we were complete total strangers, no one even acknowledged one another. No one even looked at one another. The last two weeks faded faster than any autumn leaf. Within minutes, the elastic bands that gripped us so tightly burst. This trip would not be heralded in anyone's memory. Apparently, it couldn't be forgotten quickly enough.

Despite all of the fanfare, Mr. Hudson didn't forget to preregister us at the hotel. Since there were very few taxis, I still didn't understand how he made it to the hotel before us. The last time I saw Mr. Hudson, he was fully engaged in his warrior welcome.

"Sara, here is your key and my business card. If there is anything at anytime that you or your husband need, please let me know, perhaps another tour." With flushed cheeks, Mr. Hudson gulped quickly at his own suggestion. I almost dropped the key.

"Just get home safely where you belong and don't go on any more trips by yourself. Sara, an imagination is a wonderful thing, but sometimes it has to be reigned in."

I heard clearly what Mr. Hudson didn't say. He was fearful of Leon and his educated reprisals and didn't want any long-distance trouble. Shaking ever so slightly, Mr. Hudson's hand clasped mine briefly for the very last time.

I was alone at last. In my privacy, I collapsed. There was no woodsy smell and no rustic furniture. Instead my room reeked of luxury and convenience. Literally, I soaked it up with a hot steamy bath. Soothed, and refreshed, I turned on the television full blast and picked up the phone wanting to celebrate my unbelievable return with Leon.

Wanted sounds filled my ears from Texas.

"Sara, your brother was at the airport looking for you, but couldn't find you. I couldn't believe what I just heard."

"Leon, I never thought he would be there. There was just so much commotion going on at the airport with the band heralding us. The trek in the wilderness really wasn't all that bad except for the bear. I can't imagine anything going wrong from now on except maybe if I missed tomorrow's flight. But I won't."

"Bears? Sara, you are a magnet for things that are not supposed to happen. Are you absolutely certain that you were not filming part of an up and coming movie called the Terrorized Tourists? And army helicopters really rescued all of you? Sara, what is all of that noise in the background? Are you celebrating your return to civilization? Your parents have no idea of your helicopter rescue otherwise they would be here. Let's keep it that way until you get home. Please don't miss your flight. Just in case, call the operator for a wakeup call. I can't take any more drama, Sara." With Leon's concerned words awash in my mind, I succumbed to a deep sleep.

THE RETURN

THE AIRPORT WAS AWASH WITH people scurrying here and there. Watching the cultural trail mix use to be a pastime of mine, but since the trip, guessing occupations by random behavior no longer interested me. Instead, I watched the planes landing and taking off, and all I could think about were the blackened geese.

"Is this seat taken?" a polished voice inquired. It was a well- dressed, well-meaning, hurried individual. A Mr. Samas. "Are you by yourself?" the voice continued. This was exactly what I didn't need or want, a handsome meddling, confident, single man prodding me.

"No, not really." I hoped he would leave. He was rooted in his chair like a prized orchid. The more that I ignored him, the more he enjoyed it.

"My meetings were very successful yet I am relieved they are over. After five days, it takes a toll on you. If allowed, Las Vegas can deafen your core, satirizing everything you believe in. It is beyond me why people choose to live in this town. If for no other reason the heat index is 115 plus degrees." Stopping, he peered quizzically at me through his glasses. "I don't mean to stare, but aren't you one of them?"

"One of whom?"

"You know that group, the wilderness group."

"It was a tour group. A bus tour that just had some mishaps."

"So you are one of them. I thought that I recognized you." Certainly he wouldn't want to talk to one of them. He did.

"Your husband isn't with you then? Couldn't he figure anything out by himself?" He paused, as if thinking through what to say next.

"Facts make or break me. Reporting is hereditary, in my blood lines. An article about you, your group and what you experienced would be of interest. All of you survived, didn't you?" Just to see him squirm, I wanted to say no in the worst way. The boarding call stopped me.

Abruptly getting in line, I watched as weighted-down stragglers slowly followed. Ahead of me were members of a high-flying parachuting club each donning a brown leather jacket with a parachute patch embroidery, and behind me were returning Texan big game African hunters. Was this the right line? Sandwiched in between risk takers, I couldn't help but hear the numbing details about their daring escapades. My own adventures quickly paled in comparison. The curious reporter tried to catch up with me. Fate intervened.

I found myself seated beside one of the big game hunters. Suddenly I was in a sand splattered jeep packed with riffles, camouflaged gears, and trophy seekers. It was early morning, and the jungle's foliage blinded the sun's rays. Eventually, Manuel, our guide, advised us to abandon the jeep, continue on foot and develop a personal respect for the smoldering jungle.

If we wanted trophies, we would have to earn them. It was not a duck shoot. Manuel wanted us to decipher the clues: the bent underbrush, the droppings, the claw marks, and the coveted paw prints.

Looking for the clues, I fell asleep. I became the hunted and lured the hunters deeper into the jungle. I was not going to hang on anyone's wall or be walked upon. These men would be taught a lesson they would never forget. Turning on them, I backtracked and plotted how to mangle each one of them beyond recognition. Just before I got my human trophies, loud conversations woke me up.

Amidst the bragging hunters were animal activists who condemned the slaughter. Like a contagious flu, heated arguments spread throughout the plane. Scurrying up and down the aisles, the stewardess did their best to quiet the disruptions. The more they tried, the louder they got. The hunters drank more than they should have. Their language should have been left in the jungles.

Like flint to a flame, a near riot almost erupted. Out of nowhere, the co-pilot appeared and threatened the agitators with legal action. As things quieted down, members of the high-flying club proceeded to antagonize the quieted hunters with their own agenda. Claiming to be bigger risk takers, they challenged the hunters with their motto "Free air and shute-less." The hunters had enough. Fists connected and buttons popped. I couldn't believe my eyes Seventh graders had overtaken the plane.

Watching the flying fists, I heard the whisperings. "She started it. She started it all."

Wondering who they accused, I looked around. Disgusted looks, slumped figures crouched down in their seats, and anxious mothers covered their children like hens with new eggs. Cultural slurs and punches finally stopped. Fuming individuals were separated. Now, the seventh graders had to behave.

After the brawling, only coffee and juice were served. From the seat behind me I heard, "Don't turn around."

"He has a gun. He has a gun!" a child's voice cried out. Muffled screams and moans echoed down the aisle. The grey steel metal reflected in one of the side mirrors.

"No one is going anywhere from now on." The words jolted me. Maybe I never would make it home.

The flimsy curtain dividing first and second class swished slightly. It would be the perfect time for those agitated, pride-packed hormones to react. They must have heard me. Both hunters and jumpers sprung up and flung themselves at the gunman, tackling him to the ground. The gun was a plastic replica. It didn't matter. With the help of a few stripped ties, the gunman's hands were lassoed to the bottom of the metal seat as hunters sat perched atop his legs. The pretender would pay dearly for his charade.

I waited and waited for the announcement: "This is the filming of Sky Jacked or welcome to Camera in the Skies." The only thing that I heard was, "Do not get out of your seat for any reason and stay calm. Everything is under control."

Everything is under control, were they kidding? If I had an enemy, I wouldn't subject him to the nonsense on this plane. Disregarding the announcement, one lone figure got up out of his seat. The anxious reporter couldn't wait a minute longer.

On the floor sprawled next to the gunslinger was the reporter with a pad and a pen in hand, wanting to know why. His recorder had malfunctioned, but this was sensational news destined for tomorrow's headlines. He wasn't going to pass it up and documented answers the old fashioned way by writing them down.

Jittery passengers just waited and watched expecting other outbreaks anywhere on the plane. Eyes were fastened to watches. Nobody wanted to be on this plane a minute more than was absolutely necessary.

Emotionally drained, I closed my eyes and hoped for at least a chance to get off this plane. Sleep was a sedative. My request was granted as the plane lowered, preparing for landing. Story in hand, the beaming reporter returned to his seat and glowed like a July Christmas tree.

With his hands tied awkwardly to the rungs of the chair, Stew was terrified of the plane's descent. It was ironic that someone who faked terror was now really terrified. Screaming, "We are all going to die," Stew had a panic attack and couldn't breathe. To catch his breath, he needed to sit upright. No one wanted to be responsible for Stew's demise even though he deserved it.

Silencing aggression was one thing; silencing a phobia was quite another. His hands were untied. Freed, Stew apologized to everyone on the plane and attempted to explain his behavior. Receiving months of therapy in preparation for this flight, Stew still felt vulnerable even though his therapist had assured him that he was ready. Somehow, the fake gun calmed his fear and empowered him. No one listened. No one wanted to hear his excuses. Stew's therapist would be amazed to see him on the evening news, handcuffed and accused, conversing from a jail cell. So much for expensive therapy. Stew would probably spend the rest of his life in some form of required therapy behind or around bars.

As we approached the runway, the windows glowed. Sirens and fire engines were everywhere. The pilot must have radioed ahead. They were ready for us. Just like in the movies, I envisioned a swirling swat team. I was not disappointed. Yanking my cap from my bag, I quickly tucked my hair underneath it. No one would recognize me.

"Get ready to be interrogated," a man muttered under his breath. "In the air, any felony, real or intended will be prosecuted to the full extent of the law." Grueling, harassing questions didn't really concern me. No one knew who I was or where I was going. I was very wrong.

When the plane landed, all pandemonium broke lose. Men in uniform stormed the plane with guns in hand, searching, sniffing, overturning everything. They were a well-trained squadron of police dogs.

"Where is he?"

"He's over there."

"The man crying and heaving?"

"Yes, that is the one."

"There must be some mistake. We are looking for a trained killer."

"That is the one." Derailed and deflated, their bulletproof vests sank an inch on their proud peacock chests. Dumbfounded, the first trooper in line reached the identified man, picked up the toy gun, and shook his head disgustedly. The elderly trooper had left his wife's side on her birthday celebration for this dire emergency. He had better things to do with his time than to clean up after an adolescent stunt. The sight of the man revolted him. A good punch in the gut probably would have straightened him right out.

Like prized heifers, we were herded off the plane. It was all very cordial until we got to the debriefing room. Suddenly everything changed. We were the perpetrators. Our answers defined us. If our answers differed, we were drilled relentlessly over and over again until they matched. It was a derailed game show. Since it was a group effort, leaving was not an option. The group splintered.

Mimicking the troopers, the daredevils tried in vain to lighten the questioning and almost were arrested. They stopped just before they were read their civil rights. An eerie silence stifled the others. Wanting it to end, my only consolation was that I no longer sat strapped in that demented plane. Unfortunately in less than an hour, I had to board another plane. A bus ticket sounded good, but it would take the whole day to get home. Convenience won.

Finally we were escorted out of the drilling pen. An all too familiar voice stopped me.

"So you are one plane closer to home?" Mr. Samas had his story, actually two stories and would probably alter the debriefing into some type of civil liberty scandal. Why in the world was he still tailing me?

"Have you told him yet?"

"Told whom?"

"Your significant other. Your cap didn't really change anything. They have already identified you and informed your loved ones."

"I wasn't asked any personal information."

"They had the passenger list and your name was on it."

Mr. Samas was a very irritating person, and I was certain he knew it. My cap would remain where it was.

"A bowl of hot clam chowder sounds really good to me right about now. Care to join me?" Reminding me of New England winters, clam chowder was my favorite.

Losing myself in my soup, I listened half-heartedly to Mr. Samas's rambling conversation. He sounded spoiled, arrogant, with a charmed life. Evidently ever since Mr. Samas was a young child, his father expected him to become part of his newspaper empire. Without any pauses, the pieces of his life fit conveniently together. Considering my own life, I was very grateful for the huge spaces, even missing pieces that defined me.

"I would really like to meet your husband." My lower jaw dropped. My silence was misinterpreted.

"Why?"

"Just to see what kind of a guy ends up with a girl like you." The words spilled out of his mouth. Rehearsed compliments bothered me. Like a covered pot, I boiled over.

"Leon isn't anything like you. You couldn't be more different. Given no choice, he was self-made. Raised in a tiny three-room dilapidated house, Leon slept on the floor or in a flimsy bed with seven other brothers and sisters. Food was scarce, but his mother's love upheld him along with his wonderful acquiring mind. Despite being disfigured by a drunk driver when he was twenty, Leon achieved more than anyone ever expected. No one even thought that he would get out of a wheel chair.

"So you love him because he was poor and suffered?"

"No, his poverty didn't define him. Overcoming it did."

"There is nothing wrong with an established background and its privileges.

"Privileges can be roadblocks." Mr. Samas sat quietly, submerged in his thoughts. Instinctively he reached for his wallet.

"Here is a photo of my family. A family that I once had. Within a second, my mistake took them away from me. No one survived the accident except me. I would have given anything to trade places with any one of them."

My pride choked me. "I am so sorry."

His pieces now made perfect sense. Heartache trumped privilege. I couldn't help but empathize with this man camouflaged in newspaper print. He was loving, sensitive, and broken. Maybe it wasn't even his fault. Would he ever be able to forgive himself? Mr. Samas should meet Leon. They were both disguised, survivors, and blamed themselves.

Mr. Samas's heartache just reinforced my own selfishness. Would Leon ever forgive me for going off on this trip without him? No one told me I had to go; it was completely my decision. My mother's sentiments rang clear as a bicycle's bell.

"After all, how many mountains and rivers do you need to see? After a while, they all tend to look alike." She was right. They did look alike.

Mr. Samas handed me the well-worn photo. His wife was beautiful and his two children looked just like him, especially through the eyes. Very few times in my life I wanted to be transparent. This was one of those times. I wanted to tell him that everything would be all right, but it wasn't. I wanted to introduce him to the single lady at the next table, but I didn't. I wanted to bring his family back, but I couldn't.

Once again, my boarding call rescued me. I had managed to get a window seat right above the wings. Peering outside my encased window, I was thankful for our flawless lift off. Still haunted by the ghostly photo, I considered how loved ones were so easily snuffed out like blown-out, burnt birthday candles. Sometimes we were given a second chance. Distance didn't stop Leon's waiting arms from wrapping around me.

Nationally known as the poverty pocket of America, my town mirrored itself within the plane. Faces changed. Sounds changed. Two languages could be heard instead of one. The slowed pace consumed the occupants. There were no computers, no frantic business calls, and little activity of any kind except sleep. Closing my eyes, I was lured into quietness. Climbing steep mountains, rafting winding rivers, and riding on claustrophobic buses consumed me. Exhausted, I could hardly wake up.

Walking down the connecting tunnel towards the airport, I hoped Leon was at the front of the crowd. The orange sweater surprised me, but his wildly waving arms didn't. It was better than any teetering mountain, any raging river, or any limestone cliff. As I got closer, I suddenly realized that the sweater didn't belong to Leon. I should have known orange was not one of his colors. Disappointed, my dejected arms fell limply to my sides. But not for long. Heaving my luggage off the moving tow, I almost toppled over. A stranger's arms buffeted me and stopped my fall. Before I could properly thank him, he disappeared into the crowd.

"He isn't here. Don't even bother to look for him. He has left you." The words pierced me. Only a few stragglers remained. Most everyone was cheerfully greeted by someone and whisked away. Then I heard it again sounding like a distant loud speaker at a sport stadium. Why was I still hearing them? The trip was over; I was home. In my stomach, I felt a pit, an ache that would become an accustomed part of me.

Waiting for Leon was difficult. Maybe he was in a traffic jam, or stopped for gas, or just forgot. That was ridiculous. Scurrying around me, a few uptight people lugged oversized luggage suitcases up and down aisles. Arriving at their terminals, they were checked and rechecked as though their lives depended on it. Feeling guilty because no one picked me up, I thought security would probably stop me at any time. Choosing a seat away from the others, I pulled out some travel brochures and tried to be interested. I wasn't. Just then I felt a tap on my shoulder. It was the most handsome security guard that I ever saw. He only had eyes for me as he kissed me tenderly. Our fingers clasped and never let go. I was finally home and no longer alone.

THE STORM

WITH TWELVE CATS, IT SMELLED like home. With the clutter, it looked like home.

Last night, my luggage just landed next to the closest door. Unpacking gave me as much satisfaction as packing, none. This morning seemed oddly out of place: no early wake-up calls, no luggage pick up, no buses, no schedules. I didn't have to be anywhere and didn't move from my chair.

As if in a hypnotic trance, I couldn't take my eyes off the flying debris outside my draped bay window. Relentlessly, the wind tore at the trees around our house. During the night, a severe hurricane packing gusty winds blew in and was yanking at everything it could get its hands on. Some of our blossoming trees just couldn't hold on and were tossed around like match sticks. Horrified, I listened to the sleeting rain pelting the windowpane with hail. Any minute it might shatter. Everything in me wanted to wake Leon up, but I didn't. I should have.

Two elderly voices, which sounded like they came through the window pane startled me.

"She doesn't understand any of it you know."

"They never do."

"If she doesn't let us help her, it will be too late."

"It is up to her. She has to decide."

Was something uncovered in the storm's furry? I thought about the Indians and their sacred ground. But I was no longer in Indian territory. This was historic battleground area that framed the Mexican-American war. The battles were bloody and many died protecting the Alamo and surrounding territory. Did anyone really know where all of the soldiers were buried? I stopped myself. Maybe something followed me home. My explanations didn't really make much sense. The harder I tried to block the voices, the more they talked.

"You have to get yourself back on the plane if you want to be free. We can help you do that. But you must do exactly what we tell you to do."

"Go to a dark quiet place and concentrate on our voices, and we will help you."

Foolishly, I did just what they told me to do. I hurried downstairs and sat on the outer rim of the tub. Before I knew it, somehow I was back on the plane. Feeling the plane depart, I suddenly felt terribly dizzy and almost fainted. My mind whirled, and I almost got sick. It had to be some kind of mind control, but I just couldn't figure out where it was coming from.

"What are you doing on the floor? I called but couldn't find you." Leon was worried. Torn up trees were all over the yard, and I couldn't stand up. Last night all that he wanted was to get me home. Leon assumed that everything would get back to normal once I unpacked and revealed the embellished details about the heralding rescues. He couldn't have been more wrong. Sitting down beside me, Leon barely recognized me.

"I am so dizzy. I don't feel well."

"Maybe it is jet lag. You usually have trouble with planes." Urging me off the floor, Leon carefully rearranged me on an empty stool.

"Herbal tea will relax you. It will relax both of us."

Desperately, I wanted to tell Leon what I just heard but nothing came out of my mouth. The trip was over; there were no longer any excuses. No one was bothering me, I wasn't on a bus, and I wasn't worried about anything except maybe the storm. My loving, overprotective husband would never understand any of it. For now, silence was golden, deciding not to discuss what I heard or how I heard it.

Sipping my spicy tea, I felt missed, really loved, and really lucky just to have made it home. I revealed bits and pieces about what happened on the homecoming flight, and Leon just shook his head.

"Do you attract them or do they attract you?" Leon found it hard to believe that everywhere I went there was some type of disturbance or else I barely escaped with my life. My trusting nature was my undoing. The clues were still uncovered as to why all these things happened.

Most of what I told Leon about Mr. Samas was altered. He was just a reporter who wanted a story. The demise of his family on the well-worn photo was never mentioned.

Leon was a professor, an intellect. My emotional trauma just made him angry because he wasn't there to protect me.

After Leon convinced himself that I was better, he refocused on the storm and its havoc. The uprooted ragged trees needed to be replanted. Not wanting to wait, Leon wanted to call the gardener right away. But another day really wouldn't make that much difference. Knowing that I would probably go out later and replant them myself.

Something still bothered Leon. Maybe it was the hounding storm or my crazy stories, whatever it was didn't go away. Picking up purring Milky, who was covered with soft splotched brown and white fur, Leon sauntered towards his study.

It was that deepening stare in my eyes that worried him. He never saw it before. It pushed him away.

Glad to be alone again much of my conversation with Leon was stilted and uneasy. There was too much I couldn't say or didn't say. Ordinarily, Leon heard everything. The eerie silence was almost too much to bear. Tears wafted down my cheeks. Physically, I was home. Mentally, there was no home. There was no connection to anything or anyone. Needing to tell someone, I softly agonized out loud.

"I don't understand what has happened to me, and I just don't know what to do." Then she heard the arguing.

"Don't help her. She doesn't try."

"Someone has to help her."

"It doesn't have to be us."

"I am going to help her."

Numbed, I just listened. It was as if I had stumbled into another dimension that was out of bounds. Never should I have gone there. Contact was made. Voices faded in and out, all wanting to help me. I was lured into a vacuum of sound that baffled me. At first it comforted me, and then it alarmed me.

There had to be a source in the house where the sounds were coming from: a bug, a tiny radio something from the trip, probably hidden in my luggage. If there were something stuffed into my clothes, I would find it. On a mission, my search began. Pulling and stretching every item, I found nothing. Then I remembered watching a spy thriller where the seams were checked for lumps. It meant defrocking some of my clothing. With tiny scissors, I carefully made incisions into the fabrics but found nothing but extra threads. Gliding along effortlessly, the tiny scissors seemed to have a mind of their own. I stopped. Why was I cutting up expensive clothes that fit me?

One of my jackets had a stiff section in one of the seams. Putting it aside, I grabbed my luggage turned it inside out, shaking it as if it were a peach tree. There was nothing there except for a small metal object in the cloth tucked underneath the handle. Unable to dislodge it, I was certain that it wasn't supposed to be there.

A plan dashed into my mind. Crossing back and forth to Mexico, Sombra, the maid, desperately needed a luggage bag. If the bag had a bug, it wouldn't really matter since Sombra didn't understand a bit of English and her spoken Spanish was a blurred high-speed tape recorder that never stopped.

Proud as a blue ribbon winner, I relaxed completely knowing that I could get rid of the bag discretely. The jacket was also a perfect fit for Sombra, so I could give it away as well. Stowing the luggage on a cluttered shelf in the garage, I was liberated.

As soon as I got it out of the house, the sounds faded and dimmed like once brilliant autumn leaves crumpled on a sidewalk. Smiling, I couldn't wait to tell Leon everything that just happened. I should have waited.

"Sara, do you really expect me to believe this? Did you listen to what you just said? What would you do if I told you that?"

"I would want to believe you. Sometimes things are not what they seem."

"Sara, we both live logical lives. I am a professor, and you are an educator. Do you have any idea what people would say if you repeated this to anyone?"

Alarmed, Leon just stared right through me. Like fresh falling virgin snow, I quickly covered my tracks. "You know, the more that I think about it, maybe the sounds could have been anything." Leon seemed relieved, but I didn't believe a single word that just came out of my mouth.

"Sara, that sounds more like you. You can still give the luggage to Sombra as a gift but without reservations, okay?"

A soft knock on the door abruptly ended our conversation. While the drenching wind whirled around her, Sombra stood anxiously outside the door. After cleaning clothes and scrubbing floors all day, her ride never even bothered to pick her up. Sombra had nowhere else to go.

I couldn't believe my eyes. In the middle of a hurricane? The high-pitched Spanish lingo flew back and forth from irritated Sombra to wide-eyed Leon.

Inhaling the words, I recognized *gringo* and *no mas dinero*. Sombra shook with every word filled gesture. Being the token gringo, I tried to patch up misgivings with my broken Spanish while fixing hot soup.

The garage door creaked and sighed as it was whipped around by the wind. Then I remembered what would lighten Sombra's attitude. Yanking the luggage bag off the garage's shelf, I couldn't wait to get rid of the bag. Like a quieted churned up sea, Sombra's agitated words ceased as her deep brown eyes filled with tearful thankfulness. The soft supple leather was foreign to her.

When Leon saw the very expensive luggage bag, he cringed. Surely I must have forgotten that he bought it for me when we went on our honeymoon, so much for romantic sentiment.

Sombra's ride finally arrived as she pulled the newly acquired bag behind her. Clamoring into the car, she clutched the desired bag, set it carefully down beside her, and fell asleep completely exhausted.

Crossing the border with ordinary luggage was difficult enough; with expensive leather luggage, it was almost impossible. It was a routine border crossing, but the guard must have thought that Sombra stole it as he checked and rechecked every inch of it. When sounds started coming out of the luggage bag, Sombra wished that she had never taken it. The guard was beside himself and demanded an explanation. Sombra couldn't account for the noises and almost had her visa torn up. Her brother who had finally remembered to pick her up somehow convinced the border guard that it was a child's toy making the sounds.

In order to get back into Mexico, you had to get through the line successfully or you wouldn't be allowed to enter. There were many impatient crossers and time was crucial. Relenting, the guard finally let them pass by. Trembling, Sombra realized that she almost lost her home. The luggage bag was cursed. She hated it.

The phone rang, Leon's face changed many shades rapidly. Perplexed, he hung up the phone.

"Sombra doesn't want your luggage bag. It nearly destroyed her."

DETECTIVE JOSEPH

IT WAS EARLY; THE MORNING sun stirred anything and everything. Signs of the hurricane were everywhere. Twisted limbs turned this way and that. Everything looked battered, relieved that it was over. My yard was my passion, and I inspected every inch of it. Only two weeks had passed, but it might have been a hundred years. The yard was disfigured. Some of the trees and plants changed positions, and even locations. My two favorite olive trees that were once in the front yard now sat uprooted in the backyard, waiting patiently to be replanted.

Equally eager to explore outside, all twelve cats followed me. Sniffing here and there, they inspected things that moved and things that didn't. Anxious and disgruntled, the cats meowed and whined, which they never did. Their ears were Geiger counters, at attention, standing straight up, straining to hear what was inaudible.

There was heaviness in the air. Then I saw it. The luggage bag leaned casually against the garage door. Was it real? Tucked in the bag was a note scribbled in pencil, "Don't want." I panicked.

My plan had backfired badly. Reluctantly, I carried the unwanted bag back into the garage. Within minutes, there was a raspy voice.

"Did you really think that we would leave you that easily?" Refusing to answer, I was not going to talk to something that was not there.

"It doesn't matter if you talk to us or not we know your thoughts. You asked us in."

Nobody told me what I was or wasn't going to do. A real or imagined voice was not going to dictate anything to me. The bug would be found in a safe haven, a cordoned off area with restless blue uniforms.

Leon thought it was over. He was very wrong. Once again, that glazed stare peered out...Throwing the luggage bag in his lap, I begged him to search it. Sombra's parting remarks on the telephone momentarily halted him. Leon didn't even want to handle the bag, but his logic intervened. Anything to stop my ranting. Near the handle, an object seemed to protrude from within the fabric.

"I want to take it to the police station."

"Sara, don't you think your imagination is working overtime? Have you considered what you are going to tell them? You are not a spy, nor are you a federal agent. You are just a teacher, so why would anyone put a bug in your luggage?"

"I don't have any idea but with or without, you that is where I am going."

"Sara, I just can't do this. It doesn't make any sense. Let your parents take you."

Losing his mental edge, Leon just wanted to shake some logic into me. His patience evaporated. Protecting me was everything, but he didn't know how.

Before long, my curious and anxious parents arrived. Leon didn't say much on the phone except that they needed to come over. My parents were so happy to see me, but something didn't want me near them. As soon as they arrived, the voices shouted.

"Take Leon and your parents upstairs. You are not safe down here." Quickly, I herded everyone upstairs to the music room. Horrified, my mother couldn't figure out what was wrong with me. In the background, all I heard was that something dreadful was going to happen and only I could prevent it."

Sobbing hysterically, I collapsed falling on the floor. My dad tried to calm me, my frantic mother, and speechless Leon. Waiting, we all wondered what we were waiting for. Despite my wailing objections, my father abruptly announced, "I am not doing this," and walked downstairs with my mother and my husband following.

"You haven't heard all of it," Leon blurted out, "Sara wants to go to the police station." And then he slowly revealed what Sara had told him.

My father slowly sighed. My mother couldn't hold back her tears.

"Leon what has happened to Sara? Why didn't you call us sooner?"

"We can't help Sara if we all fall apart. Leon, we will take her to the police station and get to the bottom of this."

Before I knew it I was sitting in front of Detective Joseph explaining what I felt had occurred. The more I said, the more he scribbled on a notepad on his cluttered desk. When I finished, Detective Joseph was stoic as a stone.

"These are serious accusations. You don't know anything about the people you traveled with, where they reside, or anything about their family?"

"No, I don't."

"What exactly do you want me to do?"

"Check the luggage. I don't want it back." I walked out of his office. Nothing would change my mind. There was something in that bag. Lingering behind, my parents chatted briefly with Detective Joseph.

"I don't know Sara but what I just heard really alarmed me. None of it made any sense. She is angry and fighting. But I don't know what she is fighting against. Her mind is not thinking rationally. Sara seems to be in her own thriller and can't get out."

Hand in hand, my parents walked slowly behind me.

"Elsa, no matter what Sara says, we have to support her."

"Harold, where would she get those ideas?"

"It doesn't matter, the better we handle this, the sooner Sara will give it up. I know she has a good head on her shoulders and is not easily misled. On the trip, something terrible must have happened. We have to find out what happened and resolve it one way or the other. It is going to take a lot of patience, which I don't have. But Elsa, you have that patience and now you will have to use it. No more crying, no more tears. If Sara sees you upset, it will rip her apart. Do we have an agreement?"

Elsa loved Sara more than life itself. But this was not her daughter. She would have to fight to get her back. She would do it or die trying. Elsa wiped the last fallen tear from her reddened face.

Not wanting to be the center of contention, I distanced myself from everyone. No one would be hurt if I didn't allow anyone close to me.

A day, two went by and things returned to normal. The luggage bag was no longer discussed. No one spoke about the trip. I started to breathe easier and refocused on my old life.

The kitchen was a safe haven for me. I didn't know why since I hated to cook and ate sporadically. It had to be the old mahogany table and my grandfather's illuminating stain glassed lamp. While reading, I heard a distant trumpet and a war cry sounded.

"We weren't in the bag. You will never find us. We are behind the walls. You can't get at us. Unless of course, you decide to tear the walls down. We are too many, and you are too weak. We have just reassembled ourselves."

Bothered, I stuffed cotton in my ears. An unseen force lay behind the walls. Leon had to hear it. Quickly, I lured Leon into the kitchen and questioned him.

Listening, sniffing, then wishing Leon responded hungrily, "All that I hear are covered pots cooking stew and vegetables."

"Listen carefully right here next to the wall. Can't you hear them?" The anxious look on my face jarred Leon who really wanted to hear something but heard absolutely nothing. Perplexed, I just couldn't understand why Leon couldn't hear them. How was it possible for me to hear something that he didn't? Certainly someone would be able to hear them. There had to be a reason, there had to be answers. Whatever it took, I would find them.

THE PRIEST

THE MOTHER'S VOICE WAS FRANTIC. She begged him to see her daughter not knowing where else to turn.

Tilting his swivel chair back and forth, the priest shifted uneasily. He sat across the room from her in front of his solid wooden oak desk, but he still felt it. It was intense, hostile, and determined. The priest only heard about this presence but never experienced it first hand. He couldn't get away from it if he wanted to. It recognized him.

Uneasy, I wondered why the priest chose to sit so far away from me. He hardly looked at me. Something was very wrong.

"Why don't you tell me exactly what happened to you on this trip?"

So I told him about the people, the atheists and wanting to save souls. The priest cringed.

"Then you are a religious person. Are you a minister or going to seminary?"

"No. I just didn't want to waste my time on that bus without doing something."

My tears dropped. He didn't understand. Why would he?

"I can see that you are very upset. But you have to try and understand that you have stumbled into something that is strong and unyielding. It is not of this world. It does not fear God."

Then I understood what was wrong. The priest was afraid. But how could the priest, a holy man of God, be afraid? If he were reluctant, what were my chances?

Slowly, I got up to leave. "I am sorry that I have wasted your time. I just thought that you would be able to help me."

"Please sit down. It isn't that I don't want to. I don't know if I can."

A very faint voice whispered. "He isn't going to be able to help you. No one can."

"What just happened right now? Your whole face changed. Is there something that you haven't told me?" Talking about the voices with Leon was one thing, but to a priest, a complete stranger, who was visibly upset was another. Reaching inside myself for every bit of shattered confidence I told him.

"Randomly they just start and don't stop. There isn't any reason for them to say what they say. I just can't understand why this happened to me."

"So you hear things, sounds?"

"No. Voices that sound like real people. My husband can't hear them. So what does that mean?"

"Can I be frank with you? You aren't the only one who hears them. Many people do, but it just isn't discussed. No one really knows why it happens. It could be unbalanced chemicals, hormones, emotional trauma, or something else. Sara, I don't want to frighten you, but in your case I sense it is something else."

"I know, that is why I had to see you. If you can't help me, who can?"

"I will pray with you. But this is going to take a lot of prayer, a lot of perseverance, and a lot of reading and meditating in your Bible every minute that you can. Your relentless faith in God and his holy word is the only thing that will drive it away. No one can do it for you. It is too strong and won't allow anyone else to help you."

The more he spoke, the more I internalized. Crying or being afraid wasn't going to change any of it. Stressful emotions seemed to feed it and made it worse. Somehow I had to find my way back when I didn't hear things that weren't there.

As the priest entered the sanctuary, he distanced himself from me. There were replicas of the Virgin Mary and other saints. Their eyes were on us. Kneeling at the altar, we both prayed. Calmness flooded me. Thanking him, I turned to leave.

"Wait," was all that I heard. "Stand with me here at the altar." The priest placed both of his hands on my head and prayed a prayer for protection. Before he could continue, he started twitching uncontrollably, but he didn't take his hands off of my head. An intense heat rushed through my head while nausea commanded my body. Suddenly his hands dropped and he hurried out of the sanctuary.

Startled, I felt more alone than before. If a priest's hands couldn't withstand whatever it was, how was my brain supposed to? It would destroy me or empower me. Before the altar and the coveted statues I promised God that with his help, I would do whatever I had to do to get rid of the intruders.

THE PIANO STOOL
AND SPACHEY

MY VISIT WITH THE PRIEST was not discussed with anyone, not even Leon. Why would I want to alarm people? Who would believe it anyway? If someone told me what I saw, I wouldn't believe it myself. A lonely path was before me.

My joy was my music. When I practiced my piano, all uncertainty was driven away. Since I hadn't practiced for weeks, maybe that was the problem. Passion can't be neglected for very long. Sitting on the piano stool, I couldn't wait to play the Mozart piece that I had previously worked on. The sheet music wouldn't stay still and fell idly to the floor.

My legs wouldn't be still either and cramped with an icy coldness that wafted through my body. Pulling my legs up to my chest, I rocked back and forth trying to ease the shooting pain. Leon was in the next room. Calling out his name, I only heard my faint whisper.

Whatever it was would have to stop, I convinced myself. Maybe it was those inherited grueling leg cramps that my mother complained about. Without warning, it left as suddenly as it started.

As my fingers ran up and down the piano keys, my cramping legs were forgotten. Strangely, the whole room filled with rude incessant jabbering. Quiet was violated. My mind had difficulty connecting the notes. No matter how hard I tried to block it, a constant stream of conversation wouldn't stop. Jamming cotton into both of my ears, I was determined to play. If Beethoven could write a symphony without hearing it, I could play the piano with partial hearing. So I did. The stuffed cotton, which became my loyal companion, blocked the talking, and inadvertently helped me soften the notes, which I could barely hear. My music was altered but not destroyed.

From that day on, every time I sat on that piano stool, it was increasingly harder to concentrate and hear the notes. Practicing longer and longer, my frustration grew and grew. Somehow the unwanted sounds seeped through the cotton. Alternating with and without cotton, I spent more time trying to hear the notes' sounds than actually playing.

Like two competitors, my fingers danced on the keys, but my mind lagged far behind. My memorized pieces fell apart. My mind was a wind-swept town. Some songs I couldn't even play. Others I stopped in the middle unable to connect my hands. My cherished piano had become a war zone.

Leon couldn't understand how two weeks without playing could randomly destroy my innate ability, coining me, "The awesome novice." Completely frustrated, I knew Leon had no earthly idea what I was up against. How could he? If my fingers didn't fall off first, I promised myself that I would practice eight hours if necessary.

Leon noticed other things that I couldn't do. He asked me to do something and minutes later I forgot. He accused me of not listening, not caring, but honestly I couldn't remember. To close the missing gap, I wrote everything down.

Then I noticed things. Infected, my memories were no longer mine. They were filled with things that never happened or changed. My memories were put in a safe place where nothing could alter them. I refused to remember.

The voices' random conversation changed dramatically. Consumed with hatred, filth, and anger, their hidden rage erupted. Directed at members of my family, there was no intermission. Every one I ever loved was battered.

Persuading Leon that the voices were behind this wall and beneath that window, it was hide and seek with the loathsome words. Desperate, I needed Leon to hear. He heard nothing, nothing at all. Was it really possible that no one heard them except me?

Invitations were declined and excuses made. Right before Leon's very eyes, I became a chameleon. One day I was friendly and outgoing, the next day I'm withdrawn. The voices were cunning and craftily skilled. Ridiculing me, I heard degrading comments from imitated neighbors that I didn't even know. Whenever I went outside, annoyed conversation bombarded me. So I stopped admiring my beautiful yard plants and stayed strictly on the patio. One by one, bits of joy were taken from me.

Often, the dreaded p-word seeped into my mind. This paranoia had to stop, or it would unravel me completely. My ears had to break free of these imaginary voices. If my mind were saturated with negativity, there was not even elbow room for positive thoughts. The bad had to be annihilated. Like a newly selected quarterback, I formed my line of defense and kicked with everything I had.

Forcing myself to remember hiking around the Grand Canyon's rim, I no longer feared hands that might push me over. Now, that very thought seemed absurd. Instead, I focused on the great spiritual abysses.

The plight of the Indians rushed back to me. The white man violated their culture, lives, and nearly exterminated many tribes. I should never have gone on that Indian Reservation. Without thinking, I stared, offending her. The Indian guide's annoyed face still peered right through me. Was this her revenge?

Could answers be in their music? Quickly, I tore open the encased covering that enclosed the two CDs that I purchased on the Indian Reservation. As wooden flutes wafted in and out of the tribal chanting, I focused on the lyrics. Bare-backed braves rode effortlessly on painted ponies. Wolves watched. Ceremonial fires lit up the night sky. Celebrations. Mourning. Love for my deceased Indian uncle welled up in me. A whisper tried to break through the music. It was too far away. Shreds of hope were wrapped in anguish.

Something wanted me to play the CDs day and night. My spirit soared. The Indian's chanting strengthened my brokenness and soothed my prowling cats, which sniffed, pawed, and meowed at something that wasn't there. But something else was also strengthened. At first, I didn't notice. Leon noticed and hated the music. The chanting had somehow awakened the worst of the voices and the worst in me. Compulsively, I listened and couldn't turn it off. Opposing voices seemed to battle one another. Aligned with deception, I was pulled into the unyielding web of paralyzing imagination. The priest's words came back to me, *"It is crafty, shrewd and lethal."* Spachey brought me hastily back to reality.

Whimpering pitifully, Spachey, my favorite calico cat became very ill, lay motionless, and waited for me to intervene. My compulsions vanished. All of my energy was diverted to saving Spachey. I would have done anything. For any love affair, fifteen years is an awfully long time. Holding Spachey's lifeless body close to me, I suddenly remembered some very old antibiotics that were long forgotten in the garage refrigerator. Stumbling over myself, I found the aged bottle of pink goop and emptied a full syringe down Spachey's swollen throat.

Instinctively, I lay beside Spachey on the cold hard closet floor and prayed. That night, I became a prayer warrior. Something in that closet reached out to me. Something good, true, and knowing. Spachey would make it through the night. Exhausted, I closed my eyes and was awakened by the most contented *purr* I ever heard. Next to me stood Spachey who licked my cheek contentedly, wanting me just to know that she was very much alive.

For me, it was a turning point. If Spachey could heal with prayer and medicine, so could I. Even though I abhorred medicine, I took it. It quieted everything down. But the quietness came with a price. I became a blur. Like tossed eggs in a frying pan, my thoughts were scrambled. At times, I had trouble functioning. There were jungle downpours. Tears flowed down my face for no apparent reason. My happy spirit had been compromised. Without warning, dizziness and unsteadiness overtook me.

One afternoon as my knees collapsed under me, I fell hard on the patio tile, hitting my head and scraping my back on the brick wall. It was a wake-up call. The medicine was quietly killing me. The pills took their last toll. Disgustedly, I dumped them down the sink grounding them up with the disposal.

"You are in the fight for your life, and you will have to prevail spiritually if you want to free yourself. It will take perseverance, study and much prayer." The priest knew it all along. The prayer warrior was awakened.

PRAYER, FASTING AND CHURCH

NONE OF IT MADE MUCH sense. Leon couldn't sleep because he was worried about me. I couldn't sleep because I was worried about him. My ears were Geiger counters. At night, I heard every sound in the house. The air conditioners seemed to breathe, exhaling and inhaling heavily. Even the pecking wood peckers echoed in the night air. Unanswered questions crept through the whole house.

Leon's nerves were frayed. Every shadow set him on edge in the evening. He thought he saw things that weren't there. Was my condition contagious?

The patio fall had left its visible aftermath, huge swelling bruises and open cuts on my back and legs. Feeling battered, I mustered up the courage and showed Leon the carnage. He couldn't believe what he saw.

"How could you lose your balance so easily? That sort of thing happens when you are eighty not in the prime of your young life."

"It was the medicine. I thought it helped. It tried to destroy me, but instead I destroyed it."

In the worst way, Leon just wanted his wife back. Fed up, Leon did what any husband would do and took matters into his own hands. One way or the other, whatever had descended upon his home, he was going to get rid of it.

The bespeckled middle-aged minister and his dotting wife arrived right on time. Uneasiness greeted them. Like taut-twined rope, the couple was tense and preoccupied.

Leon unraveled like a thread on a worn-out sock.

"There is something in this house that doesn't belong here. My wife thought that she brought it back with her from a trip. There are sounds, shadows...unexplained things. I sensed it the night we had the hurricane."

Troubled, the minister's wife shifted uneasily in her chair. She was sensitive to things. Listening calmly, the minister reassured. The husband was at wits' end. The wife said nothing. No words were needed. Her body language was a road map. Battle scars couldn't be silenced.

"The sounds are surreal. As if someone played tapes of repeated conversation.

"My husband can't hear them. I know they aren't real." I looked away.

"The air seems heavy. Our home has been violated. We need help."

Leon sighed, unable to conceal the pain anymore. Angry tears seeped out. Surely a learned dedicated man of God would be able to help them.

Abruptly, the minister grabbed a hold of Leon's hands while his wife slowly reached for mine. After prayer, the minister got up and sprinkled holy Water in different areas of the house. It looked like marking territory, God's territory. His wife continued dabbling holy water in every corner then promptly went into the garage, out into the yard, and returned only when the bottle was empty.

Hope comes in different forms. Holy water was new to me, but anything blessed by the minister had to help. The minister had a full schedule and seemed to leave as quickly as he arrived.

Obstacles were made to be removed. Leon was certain that he could fix everything, protect, and make me feel safe once again. He couldn't.

"The air is lighter. Maybe the house just needed to be blessed. Nothing could withstand that dousing. You have never seen a house cleansed before have you? It is common in our culture." Leon studied my response.

"No, but people do things in different ways. Prayer is what we really needed. The minister almost glowed when he prayed. Some words in the prayer, I recognized but not many of them."

"His articulate Spanish spoke of the power of God and his dominion."

I was thankful that Leon shared this part of his culture with me. In any language, anything is possible with God. But I hadn't done my part. The priest said that no one could stop it except for me. Before I knew it, my life was once again completely altered. Immersed in the Bible, I craved the Word of God like a paralyzed man craved working legs. A day didn't go by that Leon and I didn't pray together.

"I never thought that I would say this, but you remind me of my mother," Leon gushed. "Everyday, my mother read the Bible and prayed for everyone and anyone who entered our house. And not just at our house. Ministering at the local jail, my mother also insisted on praying for convicts. As a family, we prayed, read the Bible and memorized verses on a regular basis. It was the memorable thread that bound us together. Humbled, I always assumed that I would be a minister but became an educator instead."

"By listening and caring, you probably helped more kids at your college than you otherwise would have. God wanted you there."

"There were many occasions when my beliefs were tested and shared. My students just knew that I was a man of God and would help them. In my office, I prayed with many of them. Years later, several former students returned and thanked me for sharing my faith with them.

"Leon you have a gift. When we pray together, there is a spiritual uplifting that binds us together. Maybe all of this happened to make us stronger so that nothing would divide us."

"Funny you should mention that. It reminds me of one of my mother's convictions, fasting for strength. Whole heartedly embracing it, she believed that your body and mind needed to do without before you experienced total healing. Mother insisted we try it. Being poor, we were already fasting. When there was food, it was devoured quickly. The first to arrive was the first to eat. *Leftovers* was not a word in our house."

"I have never met anyone or even heard of anyone who fasted. Growing up in our house there was so much food, I was usually overweight."

Fasting clung to me like a crisp laundered garment on a covered metal hanger. Was I strong enough? Thinking about fasting and actually fasting were two completely different things. Consecutive mornings went by with great intentions but by nightfall the smell of food launched me into eating frenzies. I became a piranha. Going without challenged every instinct in me.

Taking charge, I exercised in the evening so I wouldn't focus on food. Then completely exhausted, I inhaled more than twice the amount that I missed. Yet, if Leon's mother fasted, so could I.

On my first successful night, I drank ten glasses of water and two glasses of milk and inadvertently made myself sick. Oddly, the next day was much easier, and I wasn't even really hungry. It was a mind game. I played it. If I didn't think about food, see or smell it, I couldn't eat it. The third day I got terrible stomach pains. How many days were required for a fast? My body felt cleansed, my clothes were loose, and the voices faded into oblivion. Famished, I ate, and ate, and ate. Almost forgetting how to work, my poor throat had trouble swallowing. Without nourishment, my mind's gears froze.

Later that night, I awoke. Sleep was a runaway. My whole body seemed offended at the presence of food. Voices whirled left and right. Once again, my ears became bat's sonar. Coveted silence was yanked from me.

Fasting in and of itself was not going to heal me. Like a two-seater bike, it had to be in tandem with steadfast and deliberate obedience, as well as unwavering prayer and worship. Everything pointed to church.

To me, church was televised sermons. It was easier and convenient. But God wasn't interested in easy. He wasn't interested in convenience. God desired fellowship. Praying and worshipping with other Christians consumed me. Choosing a church was an adventure. Every Sunday, I sang in different pews until one Sunday I walked into a revival praise service. Hushed voices, traditional hymns, and solemn sermons usually defined most churches. Here, there were no definitions. The service was held in a huge auditorium with a prominent center stage. There was a loud band that shook attached rows of cushioned seats, and every horn and electric guitar screeched a joyful noise. Modern songs of praise and adoration were contagious. Filling the airways, I became a spirited member of God's uplifting choir.

God's presence saturated that auditorium. An overwhelming closeness closed in on me. But that was just the first thirty minutes. There was more to come. The preacher was older, well-versed, a healer. After preaching a riveting hour-long sermon, he started healing. Spellbound, I watched nervously as individuals went up for individual prayer and tottered this way and that afterwards. With bold, outstretched words, the healer affected many. Hope was a torrential downpour.

Finding this spiritual treasure chest, I wanted to share it. One Sunday I convinced my father to meet me at the church. Within five minutes, he was ready to leave. He missed the stoic solid wooden pews and hushed voices. Just a faded memory to me, I didn't.

After witnessing a downpour of many healing services, I decided to participate. Just when I felt empowered and got out of my seat, I heard a faint mocking sound in the distance.

"Where is she? Does she really think this is going to heal her? She is so deceived. Let her try. We will still be here regardless."

It was a surreal PA system. I disregarded the impromptu announcement. Not a single head turned in my direction. No one else heard anything. How could they? It wasn't real.

Undaunted, I walked with others towards the front of the stage. Being upfront was a completely different perspective. Waiting for hope, we were God's hurting soldiers. Going down the row systematically, the healer approached me and stopped.

"What is troubling you?"

"Sounds in my ears."

"Are you on medication?"

"No."

He instructed a helper to get behind me. Prayer filled my ears. Unlike others, I was a cemented flag pole and didn't totter. Wholeness surrounded me. I witnessed a powerful commitment to the Lord. Gulping cool water, I thirsted for that commitment and did anything to get it. But it wasn't easy.

Unexpectedly, it became a family affair. Up until now, my parents took a back seat. Abruptly they changed seats and climbed in right beside me. My mother took me aside.

"It is all of us or none of us. I have watched, waited, and hoped but still don't understand what has happened to you. What I do understand is that nothing in this world will separate me from you. If it wants you, it is going to have to go through me to get to you. And you know how determined and relentless I can be." I never forgot that conversation.

A far away phone rang relentlessly.

"Your mother is in the recovery room, and she wanted me to call you."

"Dad, what are you talking about? Why would mother be in a recovery room? Was she in an accident? What on earth are you talking about?"

"This is the way she wanted it done. When your mother decides on something nothing will change her mind. I tried to convince her otherwise, but it went on deaf ears. For the past six hours, she has been in the operating room."

"The what?"

"It's her heart. She didn't want any of you to worry needlessly." As waves of panic smothered me, I gulped for air.

"Where is she?" What hospital? I will be there within an hour." I didn't know who I was more angry with, my mother or my father. Surely he could have called. But no one crossed my mother. It was her way or no way. Then I didn't know who I felt more sorry for, my mother or my father. Yes, I knew her determination and insistence.

My mother and I have always had a connection. When I was younger, it was unwanted. She knew exactly what I was going to do before I even thought about doing it. I rebelled continuously. Her sixth sense alienated me. Never did I fully understand why my mother only had this connection with me. Now, I am grateful that she does. With my mother's stubbornness, my father's patience, Leon's perseverance, and God's guidance, nothing would remain that didn't belong. Love was stronger than any hate.

CHANGES

WHEN IT ALL STARTED BACK on the tour bus, I asked God to help me save souls. I had no plan of action or any spiritual backup. Just that I didn't want to waste two weeks on a bus seat perched like a lazy, contented pelican at the end of a summer pier.

After much Bible study, prayer, and meditation, I realize how ill-equipped I really was. God's treasure lay beneath the words what he really wanted me to hear. My ears opened. Revelations were bursting balloons. When I finally grasped something, another balloon rose, popping with questions. Progress wasn't always steady.

The more I understood, the less the sounds affected me. Loosening its foothold, the conversations scattered like children playing hide and seek. Instead of waiting for something to happen, I halted it. Certain situations triggered sounds. Through trial and error I recognized them.

When anyone entered the house it stoked the starved auditory fire. The air was heavier. Focusing on faces and real conversation, I ignored it. Younger people gave off more energy than others. Adjusting to the signals like traffic lights, I became aware of what visitors meant.

One morning I was caught unaware when a neighbor dropped by with a group of scouts, seeking donations. Everything urged me to go outside; I did. Conditioned to my abruptness, Leon didn't even blink when I left. Busying myself with the plants, I quickly blended in with the landscape. When the scouts left, I talked briefly with them. They were no longer an energy catalyst; they were just a group of kids trying to raise money for a good cause. A triumphant smile spread across my face. Leon glanced out the window; he smiled broadly as if he knew.

Like a high-wire act, outside became a safety net for me. God's arms embraced me in his world, the great outdoors. Stress and uncertainty faded away like the hum of a distant train on hidden tracks. Outside there were no walls, no holding pens for sounds to gather. Air separated sounds. They faded away. My childhood longing to be outdoors was rekindled.

Often at dusk I walked underneath the sunset as God's hues and colors saturated me. My workout was an unannounced performance on an earthly stage. Walking rapidly up and down evening's roads, I softly proclaimed the word of God with memorized verses. My words formed a protective hedge around me that lasted throughout the night.

It was all about change. In one way or another, everything I loved was challenged. Adapting, I changed even what I ate and drank.

There was something that didn't like the water and backed off. Everyday, I inhaled numerous glasses of water. Not only did I drink it, but I often bathed in it. The slogan "Cleanliness was next to Godliness" became my personal motto. Much to Leon's horror, the water bill increased dramatically. Leon couldn't understand what happened since he knew I didn't relish excessive bathing. Again I was glad that I didn't have to explain any of it. Feeling better and better, I found it quieter and quieter.

With the increased water intake, my habitual bad habit of sipping coffee throughout the day stopped. Caffeine was a stimulant. It affected me. Until I curtailed it, I never knew. Excessive spurts of energy somehow revitalized the unwanted imaginary sounds as well. No coffee, no spurts. But there was another spurt, an ignored spurt that needed drastic attention.

"I am glad you decaffeinated yourself. But what about your clothes?"

I couldn't believe what Leon just said. He knew how sensitive I was. "Do you mean the clothes that I don't wear?"

"Yes, those. Your dry cleaning is still wrapped up and hanging in your closet."

I didn't think Leon noticed. My appetite had soared. My once svelte figure was disfigured. Running up and down the stairs after the cats was even difficult for me. Breathing heavily, I could hardly get any air.

"They no longer fit." There I said it. When I said it, I heard it and knew I had to change.

Determined that those clothes in my closet were going to be unwrapped, I started the assault. Sweets, spicy food, creamy sauces, bread and anything white was forbidden. It was an everyday uphill battle. Battling against myself was difficult. Chilled water numbed my cravings. When my weight finally dropped there was a significant change also with my hearing. With less body surface there was just less energy flow.

Light and darkness affected me. During the day, I was a chameleon that blended into the light. At night there was nothing to blend with. Standing out, I was target practice. If I slept, my dreams belonged to someone else. I did things that I never would do and said things that I never would say. Disturbed, often I would wake up and try to decipher these impersonal dreams. They couldn't be mine. Could my dreams be dramatically altered as well? An open window seemed to clear them up. Altering them with patience and perseverance, my dreams were once again mine.

It was a jolting phrase from a sermon that set me in motion. "You had to be broken in order to be used by the Lord." If this is what it took to get rid of whatever it was, so be it. Nothing would stop me from being used by my Lord. Once I decided that, things stopped hurting and sleep was no longer an issue. Knowing that I had to change, I embraced it. There was no desire to be who I once was.

SOUL CATCHER

IT ALL STARTED WITH LEISURE and fun and ended up deadly and damaging. Being in the wrong place at the wrong time with people who didn't understand me. Trying to save a woman's husband with the Word of God and being mistaken for a deceiver. Befriending lonely individuals who only knew darkness and wanted desperately to draw me into it. A two-week bus trip turned into years of unraveling questions and seeking answers. Who I really was and who I wasn't. That life wasn't a shortcut, quick, easy, and get it done.

With a strong, sturdy foundation, my life was built on God's words and thoughts that withstood any whirlwinds. Only when I fell deeply in love with God did my life change completely, and brokenness mended with God's might and power. I was no longer alone. It wasn't my battle but the Lords, and I gladly gave it to him. My life was in his hands, and all my tears were in his bottle. With his tears, the Lord saved my soul. Jesus was my soul catcher. Now, only his voice echoed in my ears.

Printed in the United States
By Bookmasters